Works Cited

Dawn, M. *Being Well When We're Ill*. Minneapolis: Augsburg, 2008.

Epperly, B. *Healing Worship*. Cleveland: Pilgrim, 2006.

---. *God's Touch*. Louisville: Westminster, 2001.

Dossey, L. *Healing Words*. New York: Harper Collins, 1993.

Evans, A.R. *Healing Liturgies for the Seasons of Life*. Louisville: Westminster, 2004.

---. *The Healing Church*. Cleveland: United Church, 1999.

Gills, J. *God's Prescription for Healing*. Lake Mary: Siloam, 2004.

Norberg, T. & Webber, R. D. *Stretch Out Your Hand*. Nashville: Upper Room, 1998.

Porterfield, A. *Healing in the History of Christianity*. Oxford: Oxford University, 2005.

The New Revised Standard Version Bible. Nashville: Abingdon, 1989.

of a

nning

can

erica
re

ISBN: 1-4241-4512-0

PUBLISHED BY PUBLISHAMERICA, LLLP

www.publishamerica.com

Baltimore

Printed in the United States of America

For
Skip, Heidi, Chris, Eric,

who, as little children, taught me to see,

and as adults, cause a smile every day.

This is the journal of a beginning of a family in the once upon a time of long ago. All the happenings are true and occurred just as written to the very best recall of the author.

The country as described is just as magnificent and awesome today as it was then. The Crandall guard station and the Sunlight ranger station are still being used by the United States Forest Service, although the houses are no longer lived in year round. The Clay Butte fire tower on the Bear Tooth highway is still open to summer visitors. The people who participated in the journal and all the adventures were bigger than life and a very real part of that country at that time.

However, so that privacy and sensitivity may be maintained, I have, with deep respect and fondness, changed the names of all but our families.

Joan Duncan—the wife and mother

Table of Contents

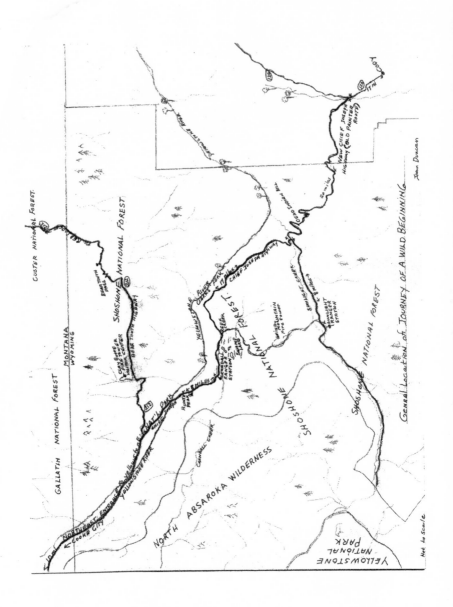

General Location of Journey of a Wild Beginning

John Duncan

Not to Scale

Part I

West to the Wilderness

A long time ago, in a different world, there was a young woman who, with her husband and young family, lived for a short time in one of the most remote and spectacular settings in the United States. For over forty years the memories of that time keep coming back as does the haunting beauty of that wild country and the humans and animals who inhabited it. As the wife, mother, and primary participant of the true genesis of the Zeller family, I decided to record the wild beginning of our family, with all its adventures, joy, laughter, tears and heartaches. I believe the two years we lived in that country and the life lessons learned, influenced all of us and laid the foundation for the kind of lives we would lead from that time on.

This was the end of a time when forest rangers rode the range, when the forest and the ponds and the skies were still filled with native species of animals and fish and birds, when the woods were empty of people, when you still had to rely on your own survival instincts and you had to pay homage to the forces of nature and deal with the unexpected. It was a time when there was a minimum of modern conveniences to come to your aid when trouble came knocking on your door. Instead, it was a time when neighbors helped neighbors, when you reached deep inside for that extra measure of strength and you learned that the very best person to call on in time of need was yourself.

Karl, who was the husband, father and precipitator of our journey, became a forest ranger on the Shoshone National Forest in the northwest corner of Wyoming in 1957. He actually was an assistant ranger and we were assigned to a guard station called Crandall. It was located about fifty-four miles from Cody, Wyoming. To get there from Cody, you traveled on a good paved road about seventeen miles and the rest was a one-lane dirt road with turnouts that went over and through some of the most primitive and magnificent country in the United States. The road was not a lot wider than a good cow path and if you met another vehicle, one of you had to back up to a wide place or a "turn-out" so the other could get by. There weren't a lot of people who lived in that rugged back country on a year-round basis or traveled that road so traffic was at a minimum. On a good day with dry roads, the drive from Crandall to Cody took about three and a half hours.

Karl had just graduated from the University of New Hampshire with a degree in wildlife management. His original plan had been to work for the Pennsylvania Fish and Game Department, but discovered that particular state department was very political, and to advance, it would have been better to "know" somebody. He had enough forestry credits to qualify for a position with the U. S. Forest Service for which he applied. Working for the Forest Service was not new to him as he had worked for them summers in Idaho while attending Moravian College in Bethlehem, Pennsylvania, where his dad was a professor and chaplain of that college.

We had both grown up in Nazareth, Pennsylvania, and Karl's brother Ger was a junior high school classmate of mine and a good friend. So I knew Mom and Pap Zeller very well by the time I was thirteen years old. I knew vaguely that Ger had an older brother named Karl but he was in college so of no interest to me! That changed when he came to a Youth Fellowship meeting at the local Moravian church where I was a faithful member even though I officially belonged to the Lutheran church. I thought he was a pretty special guy and the opportunity to invite him to go on a Girl Scout hayride presented itself not too long after that. It all began on the hayride and I was a junior in high school and he, a junior in college. Not a desirable situation as far as my mother was concerned!

In 1950, when the Korean war broke out, Karl enlisted in the Navy. For the next two years, we didn't see much of each other but the romance continued to grow via letters every day and an occasional trip home. I graduated from high school in June of 1952 and Karl and I were married on November 15. I was a very young bride but very stubborn in my determination to marry my handsome sailor. Karl Jon was born on December 16, 1953, in the Portsmouth Navel Hospital in Virginia. We lived in a tiny apartment in Virginia Beach which was reasonably close to the Oceana Naval Air Station where Karl was stationed. This was the first grandchild and Pap and Mom Zeller came immediately for a visit and to help. Pap carried the new baby around and kept telling him that he was a little "Skipper" and "the Skipper who ran this ship" and the "new Skipper," and by the time they left, the nickname was permanent.

During the last year in the Navy, which was 1954, Karl decided to finish college. The University of New Hampshire was one of the very few colleges at that time to offer a major in wildlife management. He was given some credits for his two years at Moravian so was able to get his degree in three years instead of the full four. Heidi and Chris had their beginnings in Durham, New Hampshire, although I went back to Nazareth for their births so the other grandmother (my mother) could help until I could manage on my own. Both were born in a small hospital in Northampton, PA, because it was less expensive than some of the bigger hospitals.

The GI Bill paid $120 per month for a Korean veteran to go to school. On this, Karl and I were supposed to pay tuition, books, fees, rent (we lived in college housing after the first year, which were converted Navy barracks), buy groceries, and somehow survive. I don't think we were supposed to have babies while he was in school. Wives really didn't work in those days unless it was a dire necessity (and it was) but I was pregnant with Heidi and then Chris, while Karl was in college, and we already had Skipper! Because of this, my stepfather asked, "Haven't you two figured out what's causing those kids yet? It's not in the water!"

We received financial help from both sets of grandparents, but even with that help, we were really poor and I became a real expert at making the grocery dollars stretch. A meatloaf was more oatmeal than meat and remains today one of my least favorite foods. We bought one dollar worth of gas every two weeks and of course expenses were a lot less than today, but still relative. It's interesting to know that when Karl graduated in 1957, he started at a salary of $3,750 a year and we thought that was a fortune! I believe at that time, the engineers, who seemed to get the largest starting salaries, were getting about $10,000 a year.

But those three years went quickly and at last Karl was a college graduate and we had to make the decision as to where we wanted to be. Three jobs in three different western states were offered to Karl from the Forest Service. At that time, the Forest Service was still pretty young and they needed rangers badly. When the offers came, we were delighted but had absolutely no idea where these places were other than locating the national forests on a map. Wyoming was chosen because Karl always thought it sounded like a great place and I was in love with the book by Mary O'Hara, *The Green Grass of Wyoming*. Not a very lofty decision but all the offers were in the West and since we would be living so far from our families anyway, it really didn't matter. It was so exciting and we were absolutely exhilarated! Had we known what lay ahead I wonder if our decision would have been the same.

Skipper was three and half, Heidi was two years and three months, and Chris was seven months old when we made our preparations for the western trek. Eric hadn't even been thought of and would make his appearance later. Because we had three babies, Pap Zeller decided to drive his car and pull a U-Haul which contained all our possessions (it wasn't a very big one). Our worldly posessions at that time consisted of mostly tricycles, cribs, baby stuff and toys and a few pots and pans and dishes and clothes. We had been told that our quarters would be furnished. Pap would help us make the transition to our new home. Mom Zeller couldn't come because she had the care of elderly parents who were living with them, and my folks still had young children to raise and care for.

Grammy Hahn knew that it would be a long uncomfortable

trip and she devised a way for Chris to travel more comfortably. She found a cardboard box exactly his size and cut the sides down and lined the box with a flat padded quilt. He could lie stretched out and be safe in the back seat and that would also give Heidi more freedom and room to move about. Skip would ride with Pap and Karl would drive our car with me, Heidi, and Chris. No car seats in those days.

So off we went and it was a long, hard, miserable trip. The interstates were just coming into being and although part of Interstate 80 was completed and the Pennsylvania Turnpike was in existence, there were days and days when we traveled on old Route 6, which was a two-lane blacktop road that went up hill and down dale through one little town after another. Rarely could we go fifty mph—usually it was about forty-five.

There were no motels as we know them today but we would find "tourist cabins," which were little individual cabins with sometimes no hot water and just a bathroom and beds, with no facilities for babies. Along with no car seats there was no such thing as a disposable diaper. Chris still had to have his milk in a bottle and keeping the bottles clean and milk available and fresh was difficult, although we did have a cooler. At night I would wash diapers as best I could and drape them everywhere hoping they would be dry by morning. Sometimes they weren't, as this was June, and Illinois and Iowa and Missouri could all be pretty humid and hot. No air conditioning either and there were times when Heidi would be so wet and hot, she would just whimper. We had water but no way to keep it cool for very long. I would wipe faces with a damp cloth and the evaporation would help some.

Restaurants weren't as numerous either and we had to plan our stops at the end of the day to coincide, not only with a tourist cabin, but also where we hoped there would be a café or diner where we could feed everyone dinner before bedtime. Sometimes our choices were very limited and the food was barely edible. Then we would give the kids a snack in the morning to fend off their hunger until we could find a decent restaurant to have breakfast. Chris had his bottle and I had plenty of Gerber's baby food with us so he was just fine. We had the minimal ingredients for sandwiches at lunchtime and Pap and Skip, leading the way, would find a shade tree or a little park by the side of the road for a lunch break. These stops were the highlight of our day as the kids could run and jump and work off some of their energy, and after lunch, it didn't take very long for them to get drowsy and bored and drift off to sleep.

On one particularly hot and humid day, we finally stopped at a tourist cabin somewhere in the Midwest, a little earlier than usual, so we could rest, take baths and do some washing. It wasn't the cleanest looking place and kind of dark but it was such a relief to quit moving and get out of the sun. But in a few minutes, Chris started to fret and cry and Heidi became hysterical, pulling at her hair frantically, and I realized at the same time that we were all being eaten alive by mosquitoes! The cabin was full of them and as we ran out, Skip and Pap were coming out of theirs with the same complaint! It was horrible. Karl and Pap were able to get some spray from the owner and we were able to get rid of them and finally get some rest.

On we went. The routine was always the same day after day and long mile after long mile. It wasn't the covered wagon days but there were times when I could definitely relate to that time! But along with the misery was the scary excitement and happiness that we were on our way to a new life. We had no idea what would be waiting for us and had been told we would live on a secluded ranger station. We had no idea what "secluded" referred to and were to find out it was meant in the purest sense.

Karl had also been told that he would be working with horses. I was the one who loved to ride and be around them but Karl didn't know much more than how to climb on. He realized he better get a little knowledge on that subject so part of our preparation for the journey was to visit Aunt Gladys and Uncle Max's little farm in Pennsylvania where they had a Tennessee Walker named Bingo and a Shetland pony. My grandfather and Uncle Max gave Karl some valuable pointers on horsemanship and what horses needed to keep them in good shape.

As we traveled the endless slow miles I knew Karl had to be filled with his own doubts and fears as to what lay ahead. He was a very young man with a growing family and a lot of responsibilities. Would he be able to adequately perform the duties expected of him as a forest ranger plus protect and care for me and his little children? I knew him to be very conscientious and hardworking. I also knew that he was concerned about the fact that graduating from college cum laude and working and studying so hard for all those years did not prepare him for whatever demands the Forest Service would make. That would all have to be learned on the job on a day-by-day basis.

As I thought about the trials ahead for this person who I loved so very much, I promised myself that I would support him and take on whatever was necessary to make this transition for him as easy and pleasant as possible. I knew that we had already established my job description while he was in college. He had a difficult time studying when there was noise and confusion, so when it was exam time and he had to study during the day, he would retreat to our bedroom, shut the door, and I would keep the young ones quiet and out of his "hair" for as long as needed. Since they went to bed fairly early in the evening, he could study after they were asleep. I knew that I would have to keep our new home running smoothly so he could concentrate on giving his new career his very best.

After six and a half long miserable hot days we finally got to Cody, Wyoming. Today that distance can be traveled by car in about three and a half days with planned stops along the way in beautiful motels with all the comforts of home and excellent restaurants everywhere! We found Cody to be a dusty little town with gravel streets but there did seem to be a variety of shops. Karl reported to the supervisor's office and got directions on how to get to the ranger station. When we found it was going to be another three-plus-hour drive, it was almost too much! I didn't think I could subject the kids or me to another minute of misery! We were absolutely exhausted but were told we needed to get groceries before we headed out as it was a long way back to town and we might not be coming back into Cody for a while. This added yet another hour to our already long day. I had no idea where we were going and what we would need but my brain finally was able to make a list of what I hoped would be adequate to feed us for at least a couple of days. At this point I was tired to the bone, cranky, and my recent resolve to be a good supportive wife was somewhat diminished. I was not too sure we had made a very wise decision. What were we facing? Would we be able to properly take care of these little guys who so relied on Mom and Dad for security and comfort?

But once we left the seventeen miles of the main highway and started up Dead Indian Hill toward the mountains, the beauty of that country was so overwhelming that I knew, with a heartfelt certainty that came from deep inside, this land would become mine. Even though I was born and raised in a small town in eastern Pennsylvania, I was no stranger to the woods, or wildlife, guns and hunting. I had a deep love and appreciation for the beauty of the land and the mountains. But never in my wildest dreams had I ever visualized country as wild and primitive and magnificent as the Crandall/Sunlight country. Then and there I fell in love with the Rocky Mountains of the West, and that love continues fifty years later.

The country was incredibly beautiful with tall mountain peaks covered with snow, big fir and spruce trees, huge open meadows ringed by aspen trees with deep grass and lots of streams and ponds full of trout. There was wildlife everywhere! There were huge swampy lakes with prehistoric-looking moose calmly munching on the weeds and grasses they pulled from under the water. Swimming noisily around them were Canada geese and ducks of every description from little to big, and plain to gorgeous. At the end of the ponds usually beaver could be found working industriously to build their dams, making them even higher and the water deeper. Chewed off stumps of trees left from the beavers' teeth surrounded the ponds, but this allowed more sunshine and the grass grew even thicker and taller.

The deep woods were filled with a myriad of wild animals such as elk, deer, pine martins, weasels, rabbits and the smallest creatures like the squirrel, deer mouse, and chipmunks. The sky was filled with a great variety of birds from the littlest wrens and sparrows flitting in and out of the dense bushes to the colorful bluebirds, woodpeckers, songbirds, crows and ravens and the high-flying hawks, the magnificent golden eagles and an occasional bald eagle. Coyotes were at home wherever there was food to be found and at night, every night, they would sing their songs of friendship and brotherhood to each other. But by far, the most spectacular animal to be found in this magnificent country was the bear. Both grizzly and black bears were here but the grizzly was "lord of all he surveyed"! Like the coyote, he could be found wherever food and his own meandering took him, from the highest mountain open meadows to the deepest and darkest forest glades.

On the long slow ride from Cody, as the road got narrower and rougher and civilization receded farther and farther into the distance, my expectations of a home went from a possible little house to maybe a tent if we were lucky, and certainly no electricity or running water! We saw no other vehicles, no houses, no signs of people, anywhere. We saw only the vast open country, woods and the wilderness that seemed to go on forever! Where, on this earth were we, and what madness on Karl's and my part had brought us here? My emotions alternated between high hopes and great expectations, to terrified dread and an absolute certainty that we had made a horrendous mistake!

The first sight of that little log house nestled in the clearing brought tears of relief. Here was the perfect "little house in the woods" and so much more than I ever thought we would have. The floor plan was basically square with a bedroom on each corner and a bathroom in the middle of half of the house. A small hallway with a large central heating register led to the other half, which included the big living room with its lovely rock fireplace. This room was also the dining room and had a big picture window that overlooked a good-sized covered front porch and the meadow and hills beyond. The kitchen was very modern, with plenty of cupboard space, a great range/oven and modern refrigerator. The door from the kitchen led to a landing where one could turn left and down to the basement or right and out the back door of the house. We did have electricity, hot and cold running water, a bathtub and truly all the comforts of home. The inside walls were all log except for the kitchen, and the floors were hardwood. The basement was finished with a concrete floor and the kids were to spend a lot of rainy days down there. It truly was a charming and comfy house and as I moved about and started to make it our home, I knew that we would be safe and warm and happy here. My fears and trepidation were disappearing and my demeanor was improving by the minute!

Behind the house edged on both sides by huge spruce and fir trees was a bouncy little stream called Crandall Creek. On one side of the house was a smaller log building which was the Forest Service office and garage. The house was nestled into the end of the meadow and when we stood on the front porch we could glimpse a small house at the edge of the clearing. That was where the general district assistant, his wife and little girl lived. Next to their house was the warehouse/garage which had a horse corral attached to it. There was no permanent housing for the seasonal college student employees and they lived in big floored tents in another meadow adjacent to the warehouse.

The Forest Service had quite a few horses because in that wild country, you just couldn't go very many places in a vehicle. Jeeps and four-wheel-drive vehicles just weren't as available as they became later and most of them were army surplus. This was in 1957 and that country was very primitive. The whole guard station probably covered about twenty acres and was enclosed by a fence but there were no cross fences, so the horses just wandered at will and could graze wherever they wanted. Many times their grazing brought them to the close vicinity of the house as the "yard" was their pasture and they did a satisfactory job of keeping it mowed.

Skip immediately wanted his trucks and toys unloaded and after they were located, he immediately began an earthworks project up against an electric pole right behind the house. The dirt was soft and diggable and that was his place for two years. The forest supervisor remarked on one of his visits, that if Skip's hole got too much deeper, it just might undermine the telephone pole! Skip's other main duty and project was to take his saw from his belt tool kit, which really did cut, and on a regular basis, cut down young saplings here and there. What a little boy's dream, to be able to walk into the woods and cut down any bush or sapling and nobody minded!

We had only been there a few days and were getting settled and starting to feel right at home when, one morning, Skip couldn't find his teddy bear. Now this bear was quite large and not easy to lose—about twenty-four inches, brown and stuffed, with a plastic nose and two sewed-on button eyes that rolled when he was turned this way and that. We all searched round the house, in the willows that lined the road, behind the garage and just everywhere. I was annoyed that he hadn't put his bear away the night before. But Pap said that he remembered quite well that the teddy had been tucked into a box on the front porch with some other toys that were still there.

All our searching did no good and we couldn't explain the mysterious disappearance to a really upset three-year-old who had lost his buddy. So our dear Pap decided that it was a good time to take Skip and Heidi for a walk to throw rocks in Crandall Creek. In about ten minutes we heard Pap yelling for us to come see! Karl and I tore out the back door and there was Pap carrying the teddy bear with Skip and Heidi giggling and skipping along in sheer delight! The teddy had been found about three hundred feet back in the woods just lying there. How had he gotten there? The mystery deepened even more until Pap got to looking at the claw marks down the front and back of the stuffed animal. Teddy also had teeth marks on his head, a crushed nose and his body stuffing was somewhat rearranged. An honest-to-goodness live bear had come up on the porch, taken Teddy, carried him off into the woods, sampled him to see if he was good to eat, tumbled him around a bit and when he determined it wasn't of any use as a snack, just dropped him and went on. That was our first experience with a bear in our Wyoming wilderness!

Bears were the reason our garbage pit was a deep hole dug into the ground with a large circular metal lid on top that locked. Bears are notorious for being able to open just about any container that has food in it. This ranger district, called the Clark's Fork District, backed to Yellowstone Park which was about eight miles away as the crow flies, but the northeast entrance to the park at Silver Gate, Montana, was about twenty miles by car. The ranger on our district, who was Karl's immediate boss and who I'll call John, claimed that Yellowstone Park dumped their "bad" bears on this district of the Shoshone National Forest. Said it was mighty funny that when you were out in your truck and stopped along the road to eat your lunch miles from nowhere, that a bear would come out of the woods right up to the truck window looking for a handout!

John, who was about six feet three inches tall, had the build and the look of everybody's idea of Abe Lincoln. Skinny as a beanpole and homely as a mud fence with a beautiful smile, he was a legend in his own right. He rarely rode a horse when he went into the back country, and always said he could make better time on foot with just a pack horse if he needed to take groceries along. The summer before we arrived in that country was a bad fire season and there were several fairly good-size fires burning at one time on the district. John went from one to another, supervising the crews that were fighting the fires and trying to get a handle on each one. He went for three days and nights without any sleep and not much food. The story goes that he got out of his pickup at one of the fires, took a few steps and just fell over. The guys determined there was really nothing wrong and hauled him over to a quiet place, covered him with a tarp and after he slept about twelve hours, got up and was rarin' to go again.

John and his wife, Elly, were to give us a tremendous amount of help and advice while we were there. We might have made it on our own, but our survival would have been a lot harder and rougher. The two "greenhorns" from Pennsylvania were willing but we sure didn't know a whole lot. They had two little guys— Bret, about Skip's age, and Michael, who was a little older than Chris.

John and Elly shuddered when they remembered the circumstances of Michael's birth. Elly started having labor pains and John called the hospital in Cody for them to send an ambulance. He and Elly would meet them at the bottom and end of our road where it met the paved highway—seventeen miles from Cody. He would take her the thirty-plus miles from the Sunlight ranger stations, where they lived, in the Dodge power wagon, which was the most reliable vehicle for travel on that road. It had been raining for days and the road was really a muddy quagmire in a lot of places. Even with the chains on the power wagon, it was maddeningly slow, especially over Dead Indian Hill, which Karl and I would also come to know and respect. Luckily they didn't absolutely bog down anywhere and finally coming down off the hill they could see the flashing red lights of the ambulance waiting for them.

Their relief was short-lived however, because between them and the highway was a deep arroyo that had an old rickety bridge across it and to their horror, the bridge had been washed out! There was a good five feet of raging water between them and the ambulance. Now it was at least four hours later and Elly's pains were getting closer and closer. Ten feet separated them from the ambulance and it looked like John was going to deliver his own baby in the power wagon!

One of the firemen shouted that he had found a huge timber from the bridge and he and the two men on their side maneuvered it across the gully, at which point, Elly had to get down on all fours, in hard labor, and crawl across the plank! Slowly and carefully she inched across and two hours later their second son was born in the Cody hospital.

Having Pap with us was an immeasurable help while I was getting our new home in order. He was always so handy with a hammer and nail to put up a picture or make a minor repair or to take Skip and Heidi for a walk in the woods. He was always a happy, calm, loving person and to have him around was a true gift from heaven! He took over story time for Skip and Heidi every evening after they had their baths and were ready for bed. They were allowed to pick which book they wanted read and one would be on one side of their grandfather and one on the other. Heidi, always with her blankie and sucking on two fingers and Skip holding on to his blankie or Teddy. One of the books they particularly liked was *The Churkendoose*. It was about an animal that was part chicken, part turkey, duck, and goose that did silly things. Well, there was a fairly high peak that was easily seen from the ranger station and Pap convinced Skip and Heidi that the Churkendoose lived on Hunter Peak! But the top of the peak was just too high to climb up there and see if he was really there!

Karl was trying to get oriented to the ranger station, the vast country, and his new job, and I, with Pap's help, was setting up cribs, making beds, doing wash, cleaning, cooking, all the things a baby and two little children require. I had no dryer but

I had a fairly new wringer washer and I was of the old school anyway, who loved to hang clothes on the line because they smelled so good and fresh. Gradually, I was gaining and making that little log house into our first true home. I was delighted and content to be in that wonderful country and everywhere I looked, there was beauty. Even doing dishes at the kitchen sink, I could look out the window and see Hunter Peak and huge old trees and the eternal hills.

All of us noticed that we were very breathless whenever we would exert even the smallest amount of energy. It really was disturbing and we were wondering what was wrong although it didn't seem to affect the kids as much. Finally one of the seasonal young men told us that it was the altitude and we would get used to it in about a week. What a relief to find out we weren't getting sick. I was told that the altitude would also affect my baking and make my cakes fall, which proved to be oh so true! Another case of Elly to the rescue with her tried-and-true high-altitude recipes.

Finally it was time for Pap to go home and when Skip hugged Pap and said goodbye, he said in a small sad voice, "It's a long, long way, Pap." At that point, even though Skipper wasn't crying, his mom sure was and I think Dad had to clear his throat too. The realization that our only tie with all we had left behind in Pennsylvania, was leaving, and we would now be on our own, finally sank in. It was time for Karl and me to begin our life's road alone and I believed we were the luckiest couple in the world. All the preparation and planning and the hard years in school and no money and the long journey west was to finally culminate in this wild, hauntingly beautiful place. I was twenty-two years old, in love with my husband, my children, and the world! At that point I knew I could handle anything that came along!

Unfortunately as I was to find out, this was a very cocky, overconfident attitude!

The fact that Karl had a degree under his belt did nothing to dissuade the Forest Service from sending him to THEIR school to learn THEIR system and way of doing things. That meant that Mom and the kids were to spend a lot of weeks alone and together, on one of the most isolated ranger stations in the United States! What does one do to deal with three little kids in a totally new and foreign lifestyle? Well, a positive note had to be made that Mommy had our car all day, every day because Karl was either on a horse or had a Forest Service vehicle. And wheels were our freedom. And with wheels, she could pile the kids in the car and drive down the road about three miles to an awesome place called Swamp Lake to watch the moose and the ducks, which were always there. Swamp Lake was exactly that—a huge area of deep swamp grasses and bushes with some open water. Rising straight up on one side of the lake were splendid imposing cliffs. The whole place was intimidating in its grandeur and magnificence. Just wonderful!

The road ran right beside the lake and since there was virtually no traffic or people, I could let the three of them out of the car and we could walk and run on the road and throw rocks in the water and see if we could make the ducks fly, and sometimes, we could. I would usually carry Chris but he could take little steps holding on to my fingers and he loved to be out also. The moose were always too far away to be frightened by our antics and it's questionable whether they would have been anyway.

A little farther down the road was a campground and there I would build a campfire and let the little pyromaniacs throw pieces of wood and sticks on it, to their hearts' content. There were always marshmallows to roast or an occasional hotdog which was really a treat! The best part by far, though, was to put the fire out. Since the campgrounds were usually near a little stream, it took lots and lots of trips with fairly small cups (no accident) to really douse the fire. It had to be stirred with a stick to make absolutely sure no smoke was visible. I often wondered how long it may have taken a camper who got to the site after we left to start a fire in the ashy "soup" left by Skip and Heidi.

You see, it didn't take them very long to pick up on the fact that their dad was a forest ranger and worked for the Forest Service and the Forest Service had SMOKEY BEAR! For a three-year-old and a two-year-old that bear was pretty special and we learned the song immediately! With just a little prompting, their mom can sing all the verses these many years later. Kind of like Dr. Seuss's *Green Eggs and Ham*, which was the only book they had that was occasionally forbidden at nightly story time. One can only read that book so many times. *Thidwick the Moose* was also a Dr. Seuss favorite but more palatable than *Green Eggs*, which was what the kids called it.

Heidi and Skip took their dad's job pretty seriously and when they found out some of the things he was responsible for, they felt they had to help. So when we would ride the road to Sunlight or to Red Lodge, Montana, or to Cody, and they would see cows or horses in a field, the question would be, "Daddy, are those cows supposed to be there?" and on the very infrequent times when he would reply, "No, they really are not supposed to be there," two little kids got pretty puffed up with their importance. They would say, "Well, Daddy, I guess you have to tell those peoples to take their cows someplace else."

After Pap left to go back to Pennsylvania, things were just a little lonely for a while until my mother and stepfather (Grandpop), sister Kathy, and brother, Jesse, came for a visit. They had been to a Lion's Club convention in San Francisco and had done an extensive trip through the West on the way out and planned to come see our new home on the way back.

Grandpop had one of his great save-money ideas while they were in California. Instead of paying all that money for hotels and restaurants, they would camp all the way back to Pennsylvania! So this necessitated buying absolutely everything anyone could possibly want or need for camping! Since Grandpop only bought the best, this added up to quite a few dollars and one had to wonder whether much money was "saved." He did overlook one little detail, however. The first night they set up the tent and all crawled into their sleeping bags, there was someone missing. Grammy Hahn announced that she would sleep just fine in her sleeping bag in the car! As far as I know, she never did sleep in the tent. My mother was always a good sport but had very definite ideas about what she would and wouldn't do. In known bear country, she felt much more secure in a closed vehicle.

At any rate, in 1956 Grandpop had bought a brand-new Oldsmobile 98, especially for this trip, and this was the man that kept his cars so clean, he could take a white handkerchief and wipe an occasional smudge. To get to Crandall they had to come the way everyone did, over Dead Indian on a very dusty road loaded down with camping gear. When they came down the little hill into the ranger station, the color of the car was obscured by dust, the tent and camp chairs were on top, and there was a canvas water bottle hanging from the radiator! I laughed so hard I could hardly give everyone a welcome hug! That still has to be one of the most incongruous ventures that Grandpop ever devised but he didn't think it was funny and to be fair, I have to report, they did camp all the way home!

One form of entertainment, which the locals told us about, was to drive down the road several miles and then off on a side road to a hidden meadow where the local ranchers and the ranger station dumped its garbage. The bears came every evening. We could sit in the car and watch a world-class show put on by the resident bruins of the Clark's Fork district. They cavorted and played and rummaged, ran and jumped and boxed and cuffed each other and just had a high old time—the adults, the young ones and even this year's babies. The Zeller young ones couldn't get enough and giggled and laughed that wonderful deep belly laugh that only young children have. Remember again, that this was 1957, environmentalists were non-existent, and we didn't even think about the fact that this might not be so great for the bears in the long run. If only we had taken some pictures.

We were there one evening with Mother, Roy, Kathy and Jesse, all packed into one vehicle having a great time watching our favorite wildlife show, when the sky became an incredible sunset. Brilliant reds and golds colored the whole world and we were hushed and quiet with the magnificence of the moment. Grammy asked, in a quiet voice, "Who made that sky, kids?" and Skipper, without a second's hesitation announced, "The Forest Service!" Not quite the answer his grandmother had in mind but worth many chuckles.

Apparently Grammy Hahn decided that her grandkids needed more than just bears and woods and trees to keep them busy and happy because about a month after they left, the mailman delivered a swing set for the three of them. This started what was to become a long-distance hostility between the Sunlight/Crandall mailman and my mother, for the whole two years we lived there! The mail had to come into that country from Cody and was delivered twice a week in the summer and once a week in the winter. There were the year-round ranches in that country that had been homesteaded many years ago and these families had a right to get their mail delivered also. The mailman, who was a really great guy, had no objection to bringing an occasional gallon of fresh milk or medicine, a part to repair a vehicle, and other needs. So when he, by law, had to deliver a swing set, it sort of used up all the available room he had on his truck.

Which was bad enough in the summer when he could use a truck. As soon as the snow fell in any depth, he had to use an army surplus vehicle known as a "Bombardier"—a kind of tube-shaped airplane without wings on actual skis. It had a fair amount of room but was certainly smaller and more confined than a truck. It was the beginning version of our modern snow cat. Since Mother loved her grandkids, there was no way they weren't going to get Christmas gifts and it was an absolute nightmare for the mailman! We pleaded with her but sometimes she just couldn't resist and by law, he had to deliver the packages. We weren't high on his list of favorite people.

After living in apartments and temporary housing for the four years we were married, to have our own house, albeit Forest Service and we did pay a nominal rent to Uncle Sam, it was a sort of paradise to be where there were hardly any other people. Because we were so alone, it was too hard to resist the temptation to strip the kids of all their clothes and let them run naked outside occasionally. What fun that was! To watch them experience a soft clean breeze nuzzle every part of their little bodies. They would get absolutely silly because it just felt SO great. Even Chris would be stark naked, clutching both my index fingers with his hands and we would "walk" with bare feet on the grass and dirt and he would giggle too. I continued to do this after Eric was born and until we moved back to civilization. Since we lived in the woods, it was all right for Heidi to pick a flower when she saw one or if Skip wanted to saw down a tree wearing his "tool" kit, that was acceptable also.

The fascination and love Heidi has always had for horses began that summer. Although she was only two years old, whenever the horses appeared on their grazing circuit, her face would light up and she would beg to "go see the horsies." I would take her by the hand and we would walk up to them and then lift her up so she could touch their faces and talk to them. It was never long enough and when she got to sit on their backs or we could give her an occasional ride, she was ecstatic. Most of the time it was enough just to see them and she would sit on the front porch with her "blankie" clutched tight, sucking on her index and middle finger and watch for as long as they grazed in front of the house. She was content.

One bright sunny day, I had Chris with me at the clothesline hanging up clothes and Skip was happily undermining the electric pole with his trucks and suddenly I realized Heidi was not in sight. I walked around to the front of the house and sure enough, there were the horses and there was Heidi with her blankie clutched in one arm, fingers in her mouth, and the other arm wrapped around the hind leg of one of the horses who had his head down and was calmly munching grass.

What to do? I called very softly, "Heidi, come to Mommy." And she called back in a loud normal voice, "Hi, Mommy! This horsey is nice." He was. I walked very calmly over to where she was and was able to just pick her up and carry her away. That was the first of many times that I tried to explain to her that horses were nice animals but you had to be very careful or you could get hurt. She never could believe that if she loved them that much, that they could possibly hurt her. There were as many as twelve to fifteen horses roaming around at any given time and from then on, when they appeared, my mind would say, "There are the horses, where is Heidi?" all as one thought, and usually she had stopped whatever she was doing and was on her way to greet them. Mom had to let her touch them and then make her promise to sit on the porch steps and "just watch."

Her love was complete and it never ceased to amaze Karl and me that it was enough for her to just look at them or touch them. She was happy if she could touch a horse blanket or just play with a saddle, an old bridle, or just anything that had to do with horses. This was also the time when she started to get down on all fours and "become" a horse. She was a very smart little girl, had a fabulous vocabulary, wonderful diction, but when she played horse like that, she would whinny, rear up on her "hind legs," actually take bites of grass and buck and kick. The first time anyone ever saw her do that, I'm sure they thought we had a mentally handicapped child! But she was a normal happy kid who just happened to be absolutely unequivocally crazy about horses! This craziness was to cause other episodes in her life that caused severe rushes of adrenalin to her related adults.

I had to make quite a few adjustments in my life also. Since we were so far from Cody, and to coincide with payday, we traveled to town every two weeks for groceries and whatever else we needed…period. If I ran out of anything, I learned to make do with something else or substitute. It didn't take me very long to figure out that my grocery list better be complete and ditto anything else we might need between times. Trips to Cody took a whole day out of your life and left you absolutely exhausted by the time you got home again.

Our refrigerator only had a small freezer up above and that space was reserved for two weeks' worth of meat. So what does one do about keeping bread available for a two-week period? One learns to bake bread! This was one of the first and many valuable lessons Elly taught me. What a truly wonderful lady she was, and I'm afraid that I sometimes took advantage of her patience and kindness. I was so young, so ignorant in so many ways, and I didn't know very much except the very basics about cooking and baking. Elly was truly my savior. Always patient, always understanding, and so very gentle when she hinted that maybe it would be a good idea if I did some things just a little different and it would be so much easier. She gave me my first recipe for bread made from yeast plus clear instructions on how to proceed.

Karl, John and Ronnie (who was also a permanent resident of that country and had a Forest Service permit to graze livestock on the national forest, i.e. a permittee. He was a true cowboy and mountain man in the truest sense of the word), were visiting and having a cup of coffee at our dining room table when it was time for my first three loaves of homemade bread to come out of the oven. It smelled so good and I was so proud of what I had done. I had watched my grandmother bake bread but never dreamed I would one day be able to duplicate the feat. I opened the oven door and there they were, golden brown and done. I pulled on the rack with my potholder; it was stuck, so I pulled harder and suddenly the rack came sliding out fast and smooth, and three beautiful loaves of bread and pans went flying everywhere! Not bad for a first impression on John and Ronnie! But no harm done and the bread was the first of many more delicious loaves.

We had only been there about six weeks when Karl found out that the forest supervisor and the regional forester from Denver plus one other "higher up" were coming to the Crandall/Sunlight country and would be spending several days at Crandall. These were the big bosses of Region II! That meant that "yours truly" would be feeding them for the time they were here. There were no restaurants to go to even had they wanted to—so that meant that I had to get three little kids up in the morning and feed and dress them, then fix a man-size breakfast for the "visiting dignitaries." I will say they were really super nice and very aware of the burden they put on me. They went out of their way to visit with me and the kids and soon we felt like old friends. I remember trying to figure out what to feed them for lunch one day and didn't have enough cans of one kind of Campbell soup, so I mixed about four different kinds together that I thought might work, and got complimented on my homemade soup. Most days I packed sandwiches for them and they were gone till dinnertime.

One of the major lessons of living in that country, taught and learned by every individual who lived there, was to be able to think on your feet: to learn to be creative, make do, invent, substitute, exchange, fabricate, and design out of whatever was on hand. No apologies made or necessary, if something wasn't quite up to snuff. This was a life lesson for me and used in all phases of my existence from then on.

After the kids were put to bed in the evening and the dishes done, it was exciting just to sit and listen to these men and Karl discuss Forest Service policies and to realize that they established the guidelines on the use of millions of acres of national forests, not just the Shoshone, but all of Region II. They discussed how to fight fires more efficiently and safely. We had two fire towers on the Clark's Fork: Clay Butte, which was located off the Red Lodge Highway and accessible by car, and Windy Mountain, which was only accessible by horse or on foot. Even then, it was recognized that putting out all the fires wasn't necessarily a good thing. These men knew that fires were Mother Nature's way of keeping the forests healthy and clean and maybe the Smokey Bear "thing" wasn't really that great. In 1957 though, the Forest Service policy, originating from the public, was to put them out! It had been over forty years since over seventy lives were lost in the terrible fires of 1910, but there were still many Forest Service employees and families who had lost loved ones, who remembered, and wanted nothing to do with allowing fires to burn unchecked.

The men discussed grazing permits and how many head of cattle or cow/calf units (one mother cow and one baby) a certain area could support and for how long, so the grass on the mountain meadows and in the forests wouldn't be overgrazed. There was enormous pressure from the permittees, who were the local ranchers, to put the cattle or sheep on the forest earlier and get them off later. These grazing permits meant a lot of money in the pockets of the ranchers as they could then use their own land for raising hay or grain and not for grazing. This was one of the main reasons the Forest Service transferred their rangers fairly regularly—it was too easy to become friends when you all depended on each other, especially in that country—and say "what the heck, it won't hurt for him to put his cattle on a week early."

The road that started from the Cody highway, climbed over Dead Indian Hill and down to the Sunlight ranger station turnoff, and then over to Crandall and on to where it intersected the Red Lodge, Montana, highway, was maintained by the Forest Service. They ran the maintainer (road grader) twice a summer, and what happened between times to the road, was just what happened. The road was not more than two distinct ruts most of the time and followed the path of least resistance through and over that country. It was also the ONLY road in that country. Dead Indian Hill was more of a low mountain than a hill and the top of it was an open bald ridge that had to be traversed without aid of any trees or shelter. The wind blew constantly and it was vicious whether going up or down or coming from north and south, and unless it was completely and totally dry, you found yourself praying that you would negotiate it without mishap. The view from the top was magnificent, especially toward the west and the Sunlight country—the open vista contained the mountains in Yellowstone Park. To the east, the canyon of the Clark's Fork River always roaring and tumbling—really beautiful and breathtaking.

There was also a Forest Service-maintained phone line that ran along the road, and when it went out, it was up to Karl or John to put their climbers on, climb the pole and fix the problem. All the people in both valleys depended on that line and John told us about "old Betty," who was about eighty years old, in great health, and whose family had homesteaded that country. As far as she was concerned, all of us were "damn foreigners," that country belonged to her, and whatever went on in it was her business! Our phones were the old wooden boxes mounted on the wall and you cranked out the rings for whoever it was you were trying to reach. The operator to the outside world was in Cody and her ring was one long. Whenever the phone rang, it was so many longs and so many shorts, and Betty knew who had how many rings. The line was completely open, so if you picked up, you could hear the conversation from both sides. Well, Betty must have decided most of the calls were her business and usually, when you were on the phone, you could hear breathing and pretty much know who it was. There were about twelve families in the Crandall country and probably that many in the Sunlight basin. One time during a fire, so many people picked it up to find out what was going on, the rangers couldn't hear each other, John got disgusted, and yelled at the top of his voice for "everybody to hang up" so they could fight the fire!

The relationship between the Forest Service and the

Wyoming Fish and Game Department, who managed the wildlife, was also a cooperative venture. The locals, some of whom were real characters and whose ancestors not too far back had homesteaded that country, felt that the game was theirs to take whenever they needed food on the table. Therefore, hunting season was pretty much ignored. The game warden looked the other way and so did John and Karl as they knew none of it went to waste. The irony was that some of these same ranchers were guides and took hunters from all over the United States out during the hunting seasons and strictly abided by the law during that time. It was only they, as the self-appointed "caretakers" of the wild game in that country, that didn't have to obey the hunting laws!

Far into the night these men talked and told tales of hunting, fishing, wild animals, fires, and always they came back to how best to mange the forests to get the most beneficial use through timber sales, recreational use, grazing permits, mining claims, how to take care of the watershed and basically, how best to do their job. They discussed the future of the forests and changing policies and recognized even then, that the demand by the public for more and more uses would be a future consideration. Through all of this, the heartwarming underlying tone emanating from these men was their love and appreciation for the beauty and the wildness of these lands and a deep and honest desire to preserve and protect them.

The last evening they were there, at some point, the talk turned to our road again and how impassible it could become at various times, and of course, in the winter, you were snowed in whether you lived at Crandall or Sunlight. The winter before, an older man at Sunlight developed appendicitis and because of the weather, no helicopter could land and the mailman's bombardier was broken down, so John and Ronnie put him on a toboggan and snowshoed up over Dead Indian Hill and down to the highway to an ambulance, but when they got there he was dead. We were learning that this country had to be respected and could be deadly.

As the evening wore on, the talk turned to the old army surplus Dodge power wagon that the Forest Service owned and how it had to be winched to get over and through some of the roughest places on these terrible roads. Well, I had been sitting quietly (and should have stayed that way), but at this point I remarked very brightly, "I've never ridden in a winch"! Karl cringed, the men laughed and then kindly explained to me what a winch was. We were to learn later just how handy an apparatus it was. I was learning, but had a long way to go...

Karl came home one evening and called Skip and Heidi to "come quick!" They came tearing around the corner and Karl opened the door of the truck to let a really cute medium-size long-haired dog jump out. She ran to the kids and they had a ball petting her and talking to her! "Can we keep her?" was the question and Dad said they could. One of the permittees gave her to us and we thought that was a really thoughtful gift until we found out in the next few days that she was not only the most worthless dog in the world but she was also pregnant! Some rancher was "tee-heeing" when Karl took her. I think she was either badly inbred or had been mistreated, as her tail was always between her legs and when we tried to pet her, she cringed or rolled over on her back with four feet in the air. The kids named her "Bitsy" and when they would call, "Here, Bitsy! Here, Bitsy!" she would belly crawl to them and, of course, they thought that was hilarious and would go into gales of laughter over the "trick" they had taught Bitsy. Really a pretty poor excuse for a dog, but Skip and Heidi thought she was wonderful and loved her to pieces.

She was very pregnant and not too many weeks later, around noon, I found her busy making a nest in the leaves under one of the trees and before I knew what was happening, she gave birth to a puppy! We had fixed a cardboard box in the basement with padding and old newspapers and I called Skip and Heidi and picked up the newborn, we called Bitsy, and managed to get her into the house and downstairs to the box where she settled right in. I thought this would be a good lesson on life for the kids so I told them to watch and they would see another puppy born and "No," they couldn't hold the first one because the mommy had to clean it up and then feed it after the rest of the puppies arrived. But they watched and nothing happened and they were bored.

I really wanted them to see the birth process so I suggested that we eat lunch while we watched. I fixed them a sandwich and chocolate milk, which they wanted poured into a pop bottle for a "picnic." They stood there munching on their sandwiches and then they would say, "Oh, here comes another one!" and "Oh, another one just got borned!" between bites of food and swallows of chocolate milk. I didn't quite have the stomach they did but the smell and the messiness didn't bother them a bit and they were absolutely thrilled. She had four very healthy puppies and was a really good mother, but keeping the basement clean and in order till they got old enough to go out was really a very messy business and a big job. The question was what would we do with the puppies?

They were about four weeks old and sadly, that question was answered for us. We had just fixed a place for them to be outside, as the days were really warm and the nights weren't cold—a box turned on its side with old towels for blankets, to keep them warm and comfy. At this stage, they were fat, fluffy and really cute. Fred, the general district assistant that lived with his family in the little house at the end of the meadow, didn't realize they would be out and didn't think to watch for them. I'm also very sure he was watching for our little ones. He came down the little hill in his truck, around the corner and ran over three of them and killed them instantly just as he realized they were there—it just was too late. It really was a horrendous catastrophe. He felt terrible, Skip and Heidi were in hysterics, I was crying and trying to comfort the kids, plus telling Fred he couldn't help it and how could he know the puppies were out, and the whole scene was so unnerving, desolate and utterly sad. As I held both children, their hysterics gradually turned to heartsick weeping and slowly to quiet little sobs. While I held them, Fred managed to dispose of the little bodies and finally we were able to talk about and be glad that we still had one puppy, who could now get lots of love, and we still had Bitsy. So for the first time in their little lives, death reared its ugly head and had to be dealt with. They were so little and so young to see what had just happened and I couldn't keep my own tears from flowing as I tried to make some sense for them out of the hurt. And then, Skip was comforting me! "Mommy, don't cry, it'll be OK. We still have one puppy and we can play and Heidi and I can share!"

A week or so later on a sunshiny beautiful day early in the morning, Elly called and invited the kids and me to come over to Sunlight and spend the day with her and her two little boys. It had been raining for several days and we had been housebound. Karl had been gone for over a week to another school and wasn't due back for several more days, so the invitation was a very welcome one and I was really looking forward to it. I got the kids all dressed, packed diapers and bottles for Chris, made sure I had jackets for all of us (even in the summer, it could get very cold, very fast in that country). I had some cookies, water and all the "stuff" you need for little ones. Skip and Heidi had to make one dash back to their bedroom for coloring books and crayons "because it takes a long long time to go to John and Elly's." I was so excited and it felt so good to be going "somewhere."

We finally headed out the door and I had a flat tire! No fair! I wanted to go! I really was tearily frustrated and so disappointed! I had never changed a flat tire in my life and had no idea of where to begin. There were summer college students that worked out of the guard station and of course, Fred, but by this time, it was after 9 a.m., they were all gone working and no one was around. I was determined to go! I went back into the house, got the kids involved with something, went to the phone book and arbitrarily picked a gas station in Cody. When the friendly male voice said, "Hello," I explained who I was, where I was, and asked him to please explain to me how to change a tire on a 1952 Chevy sedan. So began what had to be a new experience for him and me! What a love he was! He said, "Now go out to your car and in the trunk you'll find a jack," and he went on with his instructions and would say, "Now I'll hang on till you do that." And then he would tell me that next step and I would do it and go back to the phone for the next set of instructions until I had actually changed the tire! It took quite a while and I thanked him profusely. Years later I thought back to that day and wondered how many people in addition to Betty got a chuckle out of listening to that conversation. The new assistant ranger's wife had to be sort of odd.

I called Elly and told her I had to change a tire and we were running a little late but we would be there. From Crandall to the intersection of the Sunlight Basin road was seventeen miles and then another seven to the Sunlight Ranger Station. We were off! Now I was a pretty good driver and had driven on ice and snow in Pennsylvania and New Hampshire, but that didn't prepare me at all for the slickness of the mud on Wyoming roads. But remember, I was going to GO! Well, I made it about seven miles through some really bad places weaving from side to side, but managed to keep going. Then I came to a section that I found out later, was aptly named Muddy Hill. Not a very steep one but that road was downright lubricated with grease… "I wonder if my gas station buddy could tell me how to put on chains?" …too late, and the car did a 360-degree turn in the road. I would have gone home but we were still pointed toward Sunlight and I could see no way to turn around. I was able to chug on at a very low rate of speed for another little way, then gravity and grease took over and the car slid sideways and we landed half across the road and in probably the only ditch for miles! I was going very slowly so there was hardly a bump and when we landed the ditch was just deep enough so that I couldn't drive out, however I tried.

Since it was a beautiful sunshiny day and I had plenty of munchies and water for the kids I wasn't very worried and knew there was a good probability that someone would be along sometime during the day. I was prepared for a long, long wait. I knew Elly would wonder about me eventually. The kids and I went for a walk and sang songs and played games and had a great time for about two hours. Finally, from far off in the direction of Crandall, I could hear a vehicle coming. After several minutes, up the road came the muddiest-looking jeep I had ever seen. It stopped at my car, and out climbed a portly, unkempt scruffy-looking man about sixty years old. He had on old tattered overalls, needed a shave and his straw hat looked like some animal had taken a huge bite out of the brim. There was hardly enough left to keep on his head! I gave a very friendly bright "Hello!" and he grunted. That was my hint to keep quiet. He walked around one side of the car contemplating my situation and reacted with a grunt, then he walked around the other side, very deliberately taking us all in and then said, "Well, I can't drive around you so if I'm going to get to Cody today, I guess I have to pull you out." Like he would have gone around me if he could! I said something like "I would really appreciate that." I didn't even get a grunt. Skip and Heidi were pretty excited about "the man who was going to get Mommy's car unstuck."

He got his tow chain out of the jeep and was getting ready to hook up to it when down the road from the other direction came a Forest Service green truck. It was John and what a relief to see him. He got out with a big grin on his face and said when Elly told him I was coming, he figured he better come see about me as he knew what the roads were like after a hard rain. So it didn't surprise him to see my car in the ditch. He greeted my "Good Samaritan" with a "Hi, Dick, let me help you. We'll have her out of here in no time." All he got was a grunt too. Didn't take long, the car was back on the road, and after a few words with John, Dick was on his way to Cody. John asked me if I knew who that was and when I answered in the negative, he said, "That's Dick Benton, he has a ranch up here and he's the president of one of the biggest cereal manufacturing companies in the United States." That also was my first introduction to one of the many commercial, industrial and political giants that had ranches in that remote country. I felt very foolish and embarrassed that I had gotten myself into such a predicament and asked John to please turn my car around so we could go back home. He smiled and said, "Heck, no. You've come this far and we're going the rest of the way," and he followed me to Sunlight. The roads didn't take too long to dry and were much improved for the rest of the journey. I would have to learn how to put on chains to drive in the mud!

Now we were in a routine of Karl going to work in the mornings and the kids and I with our little walks and trips up and down the Crandall country to watch moose, build fires or whatever. There was a peace and beauty in that country that made up for not too many neighbors or friends, or stores to shop, or movies to watch. I will admit, though, that sometimes I felt a real need and a longing to communicate just a little more with adults. Karl really was gone a lot and the year-round residents and permittees were pleasant and gracious but there was a reserve there that came from mistrust of the Forest Service and government entities that dictated the use of land that they had used as their own for so many years. We were outsiders and always would be, although you instinctively knew that in any emergency, they would help however they could.

The only time people from the outside happened to come to the house, happened because they made a wrong turn on the main road and got on our side road by mistake. It dead-ended right in front of the house. On the infrequent times that happened, I'll bet they were amazed at the friendliness of the ranger's wife who kept them visiting for quite a while about where they were from, where were they going and so on. They didn't know that for most of the day, my vocabulary was limited to one-syllable words, or that at any moment I could break out in song with "Mary Had a Little Lamb" or "Twinkle Twinkle Little Star"!

When Karl got home in the evening, he sometimes was met by a wife who had managed to keep her tears in check until he walked through the door and asked, "How was your day?" I would be so totally exhausted and worn out that I couldn't control the tears that rolled down my face and couldn't even answer. On those few times when I totally lost my self-control, he would just willingly take the kids and play with them while I fixed dinner uninterrupted, alone in the kitchen, with only myself to think about. After dinner, he would give the kids their baths and this was always a hilariously happy time for all of them and a lot of big splashy sounds would come from the bathroom. Then he would read a book and also interject his own version of a favorite story of theirs, which also sent Skip and Heidi into gales of laughter. When he had them tucked into bed, I would go in and we would give them their goodnight kisses and "I love you" and it wouldn't be long before they were all asleep. By this time I was totally re-energized and we would visit while I packed his lunch for the next day and after catching up on the day's events for both of us, off we would go to bed also.

Of course there was no television but we did have a radio with one station which was pretty scratchy sometimes. But we heard about the rest of the world and the latest popular tunes plus the beginnings of what was to be the country music craze. We had the record player which played the newest 33 rpm records, so Mom was able to listen to her classical music and the kids had their favorite story-time records like *The Ballad of Davy Crockett, Perry the Little Girl Squirrel, Peter and the Wolf,* and children's records with songs and other stories. Sometimes when everyone got out of bed on the "wrong side" and we were all having a bad day, I would put on a Sousa march record that I had and turn it up excessively ear-hurting loud. I would carry Chris, and Skip and Heidi would march with me, through the house, around the living room, down to the basement and back up again, so that by the time we did that once or twice, they were usually giggling and I was in better spirits also.

Every other weekend, we went to Cody for groceries and ate in a real restaurant, got a treat for the kids and enjoyed being out of the hills for a few hours. An ice cream cone and a glass of real milk became a treat for Mom and Dad also. The alternate weekend we would sometimes just stay home so the kids and Karl could enjoy each other or there was always the option of riding into Montana over the Red Lodge Highway or into Silvergate or Cooke City just for a change of scenery. We never went to Yellowstone Park! While we lived so close to the northeast entrance it never occurred to me to even suggest we go. It was never talked about or even discussed! Part of that may have been that we had most of the same animals in our own backyard plus there was some animosity between Yellowstone and the Shoshone National Forest as to why Yellowstone "bad" bears kept showing up in our country.

We were getting to know some of the Forest Service people on our trips into town. Since the supervisor's office was located in Cody, there were quite a few families who lived right in town. One of the couples whom we had gotten to know quite well and had two small children of their own, said they'd take care of the kids for a day if Karl and I wanted to get off by ourselves. Karl knew how much I liked to ride and he decided it would be a good time to go on a horseback ride that he and John had been planning, to look over an area that was under consideration for a timber sale and logging. We would leave fairly early in the morning and be back before dark.

I hadn't been on a horse for a long time and this was the first time I had the opportunity to ride one of the Forest Service horses. It felt really good to have a creaky saddle under me and a good horse that stepped out and moved right along. Although John always said that he could make better time walking than riding, he agreed to ride that day and the three of us set off. It felt absolutely wonderful not to have to concern myself with the kids for a whole day. It was a beautiful ride and except for following a few game trails here and there, we just went cross country. We climbed fairly high and saw wide-open expanses of magnificent country plus deep dark pristine woods where you knew that you had to be one of the few people that had ever come that way.

We'd had our picnic lunch, Karl and John had looked over the potential timber sale, and we were turned toward home. We rode up to a small bubbly brook with pretty dense vegetation and trees along the banks. As we urged our horses into the water, out of the woods stepped an enormous bull moose with a tremendous rack. He stopped, stood his ground and just looked at us. Our horses were startled, nervous, snorting, and doing some sidestepping, and Karl and I were just barely able to keep them from bolting. John kicked his horse and urged him right toward the moose! But instead of retreating, that big guy just came right at him but now the head was down and that mighty rack was angled directly for him and his horse! Karl and I held our breaths, not knowing what would happen, but both of us had our horses turned and ready to run if necessary. John pulled back to our side of the stream and as soon as he did, the bull turned back into the thick cover of the woods. John led us along the bank for a short distance and tried to cross again and this huge prehistoric apparition reappeared again with head and horns lowered! The bull had been following out of sight on his side of the stream and let us know that we were not going to be permitted to cross. We felt very threatened and decided we could pick an alternate route to take us home and I was more than ready.

John told us that there is some feeling by the old-timers in that country that moose are more to be feared than bears because they are harder to predict and don't seem to fear man as much as bears do. His point was just about proved not too long after that. Skip and Heidi were out riding their tricycles up and down the little hill on the road that led out and away from the house. I had all the windows open as it was a lovely, warmer-than-usual day. Chris was napping and I was cleaning and running up and down the stairs to the basement washing clothes. Suddenly their chatter turned to pure screaming terror and I tore out the back door and around the corner to the road. Here they came, Skip pedaling his trike so fast, he looked like a Walt Disney cartoon character. Heidi pushing hers and running behind it as fast as she could. Both screaming and crying, "Oh, Mommy, the HEAD! Oh, Mommy, the HEAD!" They ran to me and buried their faces in my lap and I held them tight, not knowing what was going on, listening to these sobbing children. It was obvious that they were not physically harmed and I finally got them calmed down and asked Skip to tell me what was wrong. He started to cry again, pointed in the direction of the road and said, "The HEAD, oh, the HEAD!" I said, "Show me." They each, very reluctantly, took my hand, and both still pulling back, we headed for the road.

Leaving the vicinity of the driveway to the house, you had to make a sort of a right turn, which put you on the gentle hill, that led to the little mesa on top. The right side of the road was lined with thick bushy willows. As we turned the corner and started to climb the hill, it became evident immediately what their problem was. Out of the bushes, with apparently no body, was protruding just the head of a cow moose! She was calmly munching on the willows and made no move to leave and neither did she even acknowledge that we were there. We were within ten feet of her and Skip and Heidi had been as close as five when they rode by, so she was literally right on top of them!

I explained to two little children who had never seen an animal like that, who she was, and what she was, and that she wouldn't hurt them.

But I wasn't so sure and kept an eye on her, and the kids inside for the rest of the afternoon. She wasn't at all threatening, she just wasn't going anywhere. The willows tasted good and she munched away all day. At least through the day, Skip and Heidi were able to see that she really was just an animal and they enjoyed watching her from the open windows. ("Don't bother Mommy, she's busy, go watch the moose!") How many mothers in the United States could say that? I thought it was pretty special! She was still there when Karl got home and he clapped his hands, ran at her and even banged some pot lids together, but she had established herself and just very calmly meandered here and there in that fairly small stand of willows.

Well, we had to do something. After our experience with the bull, there was no way I wanted her hanging around the house and if she came back with a calf next spring, we would really have a problem. Fred and John had told us they saw a cow (maybe this one) with a calf charge at the horses and just clear them out from a patch of willows. She then continued to chase them all over the meadow until she was satisfied they were a safe distance from her calf. Karl loaded a gun and went out to within a short distance of her and fired the high-powered rifle into the air about three times in quick succession. That did it! Her head came up and she took off up the hill and out of sight. Two days later, though, Skip and Heidi came running in the house, all excited with the big announcement that "Mommy Moose is here again!" So this time I got the rifle, made the kids watch from the window, and I went out and repeated the process. She took off but I figured one more time for good measure, so I fired three more fast shots. We never saw her again. Guess I established MY territory. It was good that I knew how to handle a gun, it came in handy occasionally.

One day Skipper came in the house and told me there was a funny kitty outside. As we went out the back door, this really emaciated and repulsive-looking animal ran by us and off toward the creek. It startled me but the glimpse that I got told me it was some kind of cat but very diseased and wild! Karl was gone and all the stories I had ever heard of rabid animals came to mind. So I got the rifle, made sure it was loaded and periodically checked Skip's earthworks to see if it had come back. I had a really uneasy feeling about that animal. It was about the size of a medium house cat.

Later that day I was in the kitchen, Chris was in his highchair, and Skip and Heidi were down in the basement playing. I heard an odd crying noise coming from outside. I took the gun and as I got to the back porch, I heard this unearthly drawn-out mewing sound. It came from the direction of the creek. I finally located just the head and part of its body behind a log. It kept up the noise and started to move toward me. As it did, I realized that this was a domestic house cat with really bad problems but wanted to be fed or petted or whatever. There was no way I wanted it near me or the kids and I raised the gun, aimed and fired. I was pretty good with a gun in those days and I shot it right in the head. It was so starved and diseased looking I was almost afraid to touch it, even with a shovel, but I did manage to get it scooped up and dumped into the dumpster. Then I built a fire over the spot where it died and bled, to sterilize the ground. Maybe a silly thing to do but I felt better. By the time I built the fire, Skip and Heidi were right there wondering, were we going to roast marshmallows?

As summer went on and the middle of July came, the wildflowers seemed to blossom overnight and everywhere we went the world had become a kaleidoscope of red and blue and purple and yellow and pink, whether we were in the dark cool woods or out in the sunshiny open meadows. The bright red/ orange paintbrush was the Wyoming state flower and it was evident everywhere! Once again, Mother Nature astounded me. She was known for her frequent garment changes, but now was at her most gaudy and brazen, too gay and showy to absorb all at one time. Our outings now became a quest by Heidi and Skip to find the most beautiful flowers. On their own, they decided that I was to receive these lovely offerings. I hadn't known that children were born with an ingrained knowledge and desire to give their mommy flowers! It seemed an almost automatic reaction, "Here, Mommy, I picked these for you!" Of course they received a hug and a "thank you." I had to caution the kids not to pick the paintbrush, which was against the law, but we now had a shortage of water glasses because the kids had placed them in every room in the house and they were filled with wildflowers. The dandelion was not neglected either, and added her gorgeous yellow to all of the bouquets.

We were all becoming more comfortable and at ease in our new surroundings. Because Karl was out and about every day seeing that the district was being run smoothly, he had numerous occasions to meet and talk with the locals who had lived and raised their families in that country for many years and lived in that country year round. Because of his initial contacts, the door was opened for me to meet these families also. After a period of casual greetings when we met on the road or at some local function, I was fortunate enough to be invited into their homes for an occasional visit and cup of coffee. Though it took a while for me to earn their trust, eventually some of them even came to my house for a visit, which made me so very proud.

Since we all had children and a few of the women had fairly young children, we had a common topic which opened the way for some friendships. While the kids played and had a great time together, we learned that women are the same the world over and always have so much in common. I'm sure that I learned so very much more from them than they did from me and their tried-and-true recipes for wild game were a great addition to my meager knowledge in the kitchen. Some of those gals were amazing seamstresses and did some truly wonderful needlework and quilting. They offered to teach me but at that time in my life I just didn't have the time or the inclination.

I did manage to reciprocate in one area. There was a young girl about ten years old whose folks had this old baby grand piano that was kept in the formal parlor of their old and beautifully constructed log house. She wanted to learn to play the piano so badly, and when her mother discovered that I had taken lessons for many years, she asked if I could maybe teach her daughter. As luck would have it, I had brought some of my music with me hoping that somewhere I might find a piano to play. The piano was very much out of tune but all the keys functioned and we started. She was a really sweet girl and did want to learn and she practiced faithfully for our once-a-week lessons. It was fun and very gratifying for me to be able to give back something of value to a family that gave us their friendship and goodwill. We continued the lessons as regularly as we could while we were at Crandall and my little friend did well.

One of the topics that arose one day concerned education. Since there was no feasible way for the children to go to school without moving to Cody for the school year, they taught them at home. The Sunlight/Crandall women with school-age children had a cooperative program that tied in with the school system in Cody, where their papers were graded and assignments sent by mail. It seemed to be a satisfactory program and they were proud of the fact that several young people from their part of the world did well and had degrees from colleges. It made me wonder how long we would be there and whether I would have to be a teacher in residence when the time came. Skip would be ready in two years, Heidi in three and Chris right behind her. I guess we would do what we needed to do. I had no way of knowing at that point whether the Forest Service would take the kids and their ages into consideration in assigning Karl his next position. Our understanding was that the previous ranger in that country had two children and they were home schooled. This whole lifestyle was getting more interesting by the minute!

Since there where times when Karl and all the men were out on work assignments all over the district and I was the only adult left at the guard station, another duty was added to my already impressive resumé. I had to learn to operate a short-wave radio! The feeling of the general public at that time was that the main purpose of the Forest Service was to put out fires! Nothing was further from the truth, but when a fire did occur, everything else stopped and all resources and manpower were directed to the fire until it was out. If a fire was reported in Cody that was identified as being on our district, I had to get on the radio and be a dispatcher. Until I got the hang of it, the men at Clay Butte and Windy Mountain couldn't resist the temptation to get me on the radio and tease me about the use of the codes. "Ten-four" was the response for "OK, I understand" and that's the only one I ever got straight. I'd usually just give it up and use regular speech. I'm sure it got boring sometimes on those towers and once they got to know me, they'd sometimes get a three-way conversation going and I'd go bonkers trying to keep track of which conversation was with whom.

In the two years we were there, when the calls came in earnest from the towers and I had to find Karl and John and act as a dispatcher and relay messages between Crandall and the supervisor's office in Cody or the ranger station at Sunlight, I always sent up a fervent prayer: "Please don't let me screw things up!" I also prayed that the kids wouldn't pick that time to have a disaster. Sometimes I had Chris balanced on my hip while I tried to do a good job. Thank goodness it only happened rarely.

Of the two towers, Windy Mountain was accessible only by foot or horseback, but Clay Butte was right off a main tourist-traveled highway to Red Lodge, Montana, and the spectacular Bear Tooth Pass. Since the tower was just a short distance off the highway, it could easily be seen by travelers and had a fair amount of visitors, even in those days.

It was classic in design and looked like everybody's idea of what a fire tower should look like. There was a fairly small enclosed little house at the base which was a one-room apartment and living quarters for whoever manned the tower. Then the huge pyramid wood framework started right over the house with crisscrossing beams for support and each level getting narrower as it rose to the top where there was a glass-enclosed square platform. This is where the ranger (usually a seasonal employee) had his or her instruments, field glasses, and spent most of the time. The stairway up wasn't much more than a ladder and had to be negotiated very carefully.

The towers were placed strategically on the highest point of land so that by the time the elevation of the tower itself was added, there was a feeling of being truly on top of the world, which was literally true, at least for that part of the country. They were designed so that whoever manned them could spot smoke as quickly as a fire started and with instruments, pinpoint its exact location, get on the radio or phone, then act as dispatcher for the crews who would fight the fire and send them directly to the fire location before the fire had a chance to grow.

The gentleman who manned Clay Butte was an older man by the name of Sam Burton—probably in his early sixties, which I thought was "old" in those days. He'd been on that tower every summer for a lot of years. He was tall and slim with gray hair, mustache very neatly trimmed, and very distinguished looking in his Forest Service uniform. He had a soft, deep kind of scratchy voice and was very articulate and businesslike until you saw the sparkle in his blue eyes. He had an extremely dry sense of humor and was ever aware of the humor to be found in almost any situation.

He enjoyed Skip and Heidi and little Chris when we visited, and they adored him. One of their favorite outings on any given weekend was "can we go see Sam?" It was exciting to visit him but part of the thrill for them was to climb all those steps. In fact it wasn't a trip I could manage by myself as the climb to the top necessitated an adult being firmly behind each child and then someone had to carry Chris up all those steps. Quite a project to get everybody up there! But it was well worth it to see the vast expanse of high peaks and wilderness and we knew the country well enough by now to recognize the Crandall guard station, Swamp Lake, Hunter Peak and some of the other landmarks.

We also enjoyed listening to Sam and his stories, which were full of humor and wit. Time after time he answered the same questions and for the most part truly enjoyed visiting with the public. He educated them about the Forest Service and what national forests were all about and was a fine public relations man for Smokey Bear. However, on two occasions that we know about, his boredom and sense of devilish humor got the best of him. One of the visitors looking through the telescope at the surrounding hills spied the many outcroppings of rimrock, and turned to Sam and asked, "Who built all those rock walls?" And Sam, without batting an eye, answered in that soft authoritative voice, "Those were built by the CCC boys when they came through this country in the late thirties."

The other story involved the latrine. As you pulled up to the tower in your car, immediately in front of the parking area, was a path that led down over a hill to the outdoor toilet which you couldn't see from the lot. There was a typical Forest Service sign labeled "Latrine," with an arrow that pointed in the right direction. I have to admit though, that it did look like it was pointing off into space. One portly gentleman arrived at the top of the tower all out of breath and demanded to know from Art, "Which one is Latrine Peak?" Art never hesitated, pointed to a far-away peak and said, "That one."

Chris, at that time, was on the small side for his age and prone to catch colds fairly easily. He was a fussy eater, although he loved his apple juice. He would wake up from a nap saying, "Uh durce, Uh durce," (meaning juice) and Pap said we had an elegant child as it sounded as though he were asking for hors d'oeuvres! Most of the time he was a really happy baby and pretty easy to please but always seemed to have a slight cold. One day during his bath, I noticed he had a fairly hard lump behind each ear. I tried to ignore them thinking they would eventually go away but after a couple of weeks decided we better see a doctor. We hadn't been to any doctors as yet, so it was pretty much a matter of picking one from the phone book, which is what we did. Why we didn't ask John or Elly to recommend a doctor, I will never know. Cody had a small hospital at that time and very adequate medical facilities for a town that size.

The day of the appointment, Karl took off work and we set off in high spirits, as we usually did when we went to town. Skip and Heidi knew there would be some kind of a treat, as there always was when we went to town. After a short wait, we went into the doctor, who was middle-aged and obviously had not been around children very much or didn't care that he was rather gruff and impatient. My first impression was not a good one. He examined Chris thoroughly. He listened, poked and prodded, not very gently sometimes, not volunteering any information as he explored our little boy, and then he said, "This could be a sign of leukemia and I have to do a biopsy!" My brain didn't want to register what I had just heard and when I looked at Karl I could see the horror in his eyes too. I silently screamed, "Please, God, not my Chris!" The tears ran down my face and I wasn't even aware of them until Skip asked why was Mommy crying? We held an upset crying baby while the doctor deadened an area and took the small specimen needed for the biopsy. Then he told us we wouldn't know anything for ten days as he had to send it to the national health center in Atlanta, Georgia, to be tested—there was no place closer. There were no words of comfort or assurance—he did his job and that was it.

As I write this so many long years later and I look at the fine healthy six-foot-two-inch man that Chris has become, I still have trouble believing that a doctor could be so callous and unfeeling. He had just told us that Chris could die and there was nothing in his voice that wasn't matter-of-fact. You have to remember that Karl and I were very young and inexperienced when it came to doctors and as far as we were concerned, they were gods and all of them deserved respect. Somehow, we got the supplies we needed, and reassured Skip and Heidi, who could certainly tell that this was not the usual fun trip to Cody. On the drive back I held Chris in my arms as he slept an exhausted sleep and the tears fell from my face onto his. Karl's hand reached for mine and his face was wet too. There was not the usual wrestling and giggling in the back seat, as Skip and Heidi could tell that all was not well. I put the three of them to bed after their usual bedtime book and then Karl and I held each other and sobbed together.

For ten days we watched that little boy, doing what we had to do automatically, in a trance, and every other thought was, "Please, God, let him be OK." Karl and I would look at each other and the tears would come unbidden. If only the doctor had given us even one little word of encouragement to help us get through those days. Finally the ten days were up and I would not let us call one day sooner. With trembling hands and Karl standing there at the phone with me, I rang the doctor's office. The nurse put us through and the doctor's voice came on still flat, gruff, and emotionless and informed us that the test had come back yesterday and Chris did not have leukemia! He went on to say that with constant colds sometimes the glands swell and it takes them a long time to go down, but I didn't pay much attention to the rest of it. He hadn't even bothered to call us the day before and tell us as soon as he knew the results! But we were so elated, we were so thankful, it didn't occur to us then that he had put us through the worst kind of hell. But the fact that our baby was fine overshadowed everything else. We could put our anguish aside and live again!

As summer moved into the end of August, it was becoming very obvious that the nights were getting pretty cool and a fire in the fireplace just didn't do the job anymore. Since Karl still had to go on periodic overnight trips, it was now time for another lesson to be learned! The house had a furnace in the basement that burned wood with a central register in the hall upstairs that heated the whole house. There was a smaller room in the basement behind the furnace that was filled with wood cut to the width of the furnace bed, but it had to be split! Karl worked very hard to keep enough split to stay way ahead of what we would need, but he wanted me to know how, in case it turned really cold suddenly or for some reason he was away longer than he thought.

For a husband to teach his wife to split wood is kind of like teaching her to drive a car…it doesn't work very well and everybody gets cranky. There is a definite knack to how you hit the wood with the axe so it will go through, kind of a last-second effort just as the axe connects with the wood. You also have to plant the axe in the wood with the first lick and lift the whole piece with the axe in it, PLUS, there is definitely a certain way to stand so that when the axe does make it through the wood it doesn't keep going right on through a leg or foot that happens to be in the way. There are the pieces that absolutely refuse to stand on end, so that requires another lesson on how to hold the axe near the blade with your right hand, balance the wood with your left, and pull your hand away the split second before the axe hits the wood. And, oh yes, there is a huge round block of wood that you stand each piece on so your axe doesn't go through the concrete floor.

My first tries with an axe were interesting to say the least. I hit the wood with the side of the axe, with the handle of the axe. I stuck the axe in the wood hard enough to make it difficult to get out but not hard enough to split it. I hit the side of my leg so hard with the (thank goodness) side of the axe that I had a bruise for weeks. I missed the wood completely and buried the blade deep into the chopping block and after each four or five tries, I would say to Karl, "Now show me again how you do this." He had already made up his mind that he better just have enough split all the time and we could just "never mind," but by now I was tearily frustrated, angry at Karl because he "just wasn't giving me the right instructions," and bound, damned, and determined to do it. My Pennsylvania Dutch stubborn kicked in and by god, I would learn how! Karl gave up and headed upstairs to check on the kids. For the umteenth millionth time, I raised the axe high, gave a mighty swing and I split a log in two! I did it! Must have been a fluke, better try again. Did it again and again and again! Then I discovered what men have known for a long time. There is a certain satisfaction to splitting wood that relaxes the mind and takes the edge off a bad day. I don't think there was ever a time when I had to split wood, but occasionally I would get the kids occupied upstairs and sneak down into the basement and split wood for the sheer satisfaction of it. Made me relaxed and I got really good at it.

September brought hunting season and Karl decided that maybe it would be a good idea for us to shoot an elk so we would have meat for the winter, or maybe it was just a new and fun thing to do. "Did I want to go elk hunting?" Of course, but I wasn't even sure what an elk looked like except maybe from pictures I had seen. We had encountered just about every other animal in that country, but as yet, no elk. Since we had three little ones, that meant that we could only hunt one at a time while the other stayed home with the kids.

Karl took his turn first and on the advice of the locals, hunted in certain areas off the main road where they told him it might be worthwhile. This was another, almost puzzling attribute of the residents in that country. They willingly shared any information they had on where game might be found. In Pennsylvania, the opposite was true. The favorite haunts of deer, pheasant, fish or any other wild game were guarded like national security secrets. But here, that information was given freely and after I pondered the reason for this, I can only guess that there was such an overabundance of game in proportion to the few hunters, that no one felt threatened. Karl's first try was unsuccessful and now it was my turn! Since I was going to hunt by myself, he took us all for a ride one evening and showed me on the south or east end of Swamp Lake, where I could park the car and walk a game trail that took off just a short distance from the road and wound through the woods and meadows at the base of the cliffs.

I had been raised with guns. All my uncles hunted and so did my grandfather, and whenever we went to their homes or to land that my grandfather owned in the Pocono Mountains of Pennsylvania, the guns went also. Part of the fun of being in the hills was that everybody, including the aunts, the cousins and even the smallest kids (with an adult helping to hold the gun), got to target practice. Gun safety was primary and there was no second chance. If you didn't do as you were told—to hold the gun properly, point in the right direction, always be aware of people around you, etc.—the gun, usually a .22, was literally yanked out of your hands with a rough "I told you!" and your shooting was over for that day!

By the time I was thirteen years old, I had bought my first gun, a single-shot .22. My allowance was usually spent on at least one box of shells. Incidentally, that .22 single-shot was bought from Karl's brother, Gerhard, for three dollars. I would take my collie, Laddie, with me and we would walk a few miles to a big patch of woods outside of Nazareth. I would take either a bonafide target with me from the hardware store (they gave them to me free when I bought a box of shells) or have a can in my pocket to attach to a tree or branch or stump. Even at this stage of my life I loved the woods, and to ramble through them with my dog and my gun was my idea of a perfect afternoon. I never was your typical female teenager.

I also had a cousin four years older than I, who lived on a 120-acre dairy farm about four miles from Nazareth. I fell in love with the farm when I was about three years old and this truly was my second home. I spent every moment there when I didn't have an obligation to be home for school, piano lessons, or whatever. My Aunt Ethel encouraged my visits and was a sweet loving influence all my life. My cousin Owen was my idol and I adored him. When I was on the farm, I was one step behind him wherever he went and if he stopped suddenly, I bumped into him. He taught me how to shoot high-powered rifles, shotguns, pistols, everything in between, and also how to refinish a gun stock and re-blue the barrel of a gun. I was his shadow, disdaining the life of the farmer's wife who took care of chickens, planted a garden and gathered eggs, which was all done by my aunt and my female cousin. I was milking cows, greasing axles on wagons and tractors, shoveling manure, and riding my beloved pony Sugarfoot. But all that is another story.

But with all that knowledge, I had never hunted for or shot anything bigger than a crow and a ruffed grouse in New Hampshire when Karl and I went hunting one fall. Now I was supposed to shoot a huge bull elk and I wasn't real sure what he looked like! Oh well, it wouldn't hurt to walk through the woods for a couple of hours and it was a soothing, relaxing diversion to get away from the kids for a while.

So one chilly morning after everyone was up and fed, we loaded the kids in the car, I was bundled up really warm, and we headed down the road to Swamp Lake. Karl let me out and pointed to the rather obvious game trail that took off through the woods. He told me to hunt through that country and he would be back to pick me up in about two hours. I had the old

Springfield army surplus rifle, a 30.06, and I felt pretty secure and sure of myself until the little green Chevy disappeared over the hill.

I stepped into the woods and the cool morning sunshine vanished. Suddenly, the huge trees and the thick woods seemed to become gloomy, foreboding and funereal. I started down the game trail very slowly and felt uneasy and very uncomfortable with where I was. For the first time since coming to Wyoming I was totally alone in the woods and all the horror stories of unpredictable moose and terrorizing bears invaded my thoughts and I panicked. I wanted to bolt back to the safety of the road and the cheery sunshine. Why did I let myself be talked into this? Then reason started to slowly take over and I convinced myself that I was a very good shot, had a gun that would do serious damage to any animal, and I couldn't disgrace myself or the new assistant ranger, who just happened to be my husband.

Besides, I did truly love the woods and wasn't afraid to be alone in them in Pennsylvania, so why should I be afraid here? From that point on I did start to concentrate on why I was there. I walked very slowly and very quietly and took stock of the terrain and where I was. The trail ran along the base of the cliffs that framed Swamp Lake and sloped gradually upward toward the cliffs. I was on fairly level ground and the land on my left climbed gently to a level bench before it went almost straight up. The woods were very thick and dense and only occasionally, where there was a grove of aspens, was the sun able to shine through and I was able to see beyond the immediate foliage. But again, my appreciation for the beauty of that country permeated my being and I wasn't aware of anywhere else on God's earth where I could feel that maybe, just maybe, I was the first person ever to step on this particular piece of dirt.

By this time I was enjoying the gorgeous fall day, not really caring or looking very hard to see if I could spot an elk. I had just entered a particularly dense and dark part of the woods when suddenly I knew without any doubt that something or someone was near. I could sense "something" as sure as I was standing there. I stopped walking, felt an adrenalin rush, became very short of breath, made sure the safety was off, and got a very firm grip on the rifle. I let my eyes scan and search every inch of the area, not knowing what I was looking for but sure that something or someone was there. Then I looked up into the thick brush and trees above the trail on that little bench, and out of the foliage materialized one of the most magnificent animals I had ever seen! No doubt it was an elk, but what a beauty! It was a huge bull with a tremendous rack. He stood sideways with his head turned just staring at me and I stared back not believing anything that beautiful even existed! The seconds seemed like hours. It was a classic pose for a classic shot and I knew it.

Some people would pay thousands of dollars and spend a lifetime for a shot like that. I also knew there was no way that I would ever in my life shoot an animal that was the absolute epitome of all that an elk could be. Maybe a younger bull or a cow but not that guy—I let his majesty go on his way and I went mine. When Karl and the kids showed up I told them I just hadn't seen anything.

Since it was a weekend and I was now more than enthused about this whole hunting business, the very next morning I got up very early and took off just walking up behind the ranger station. There was a huge area that was an old windfall with downed trees lying every which way but a little more open and brushy. Karl though it might be a good place for elk to browse. Again, it was very quiet and peaceful and this time I was relaxed and enjoying being out immensely. Game trails were everywhere and I walked slowly and quietly, ever on the alert, for any movement or any sound. As I walked and climbed over brush and dead trees, I was reminding myself that Karl told me if I shot anything, just to make sure it was dead and then to get back to the house quickly. We could then bundle the kids and all go back to the carcass and he would make sure we had the right tools to skin it, gut it, and take care of the meat.

I walked for a long time, was quite a distance from the house and had turned around and was headed back, when a shrill sharp whistle filled the air! I thought there must be other hunters nearby and since I didn't want to get shot, I yelled, "Hello, I'm over here!" at the top of my lungs. I was totally ignored and more whistles followed and I kept yelling, "I'm over here!" and nobody answered. I felt that I was in the middle of a huge bunch of hunters but I couldn't see very far because of the underbrush although I could hear movement in the trees and limbs snapping, like someone was hiking, way off in the distance. I supposed they had some kind of a system and I was going to get shot if I stayed there. I felt very edgy and threatened, got out of there, and headed quickly for home.

When I got into the house, Karl had just finished feeding the kids breakfast. I started to tell my story, was all out of breath and excited and the words were tumbling over each other. It was obvious that I was annoyed because those hunters wouldn't answer me, and Karl started to laugh and wouldn't quit and I got madder and even more upset and then he informed me when he could catch his breath, that what I heard were elk bugling to each other! It was mating season and that's how they courted the females and let them know they were around and available! Another lesson learned and another opportunity missed—but this was getting to be fun!

Karl did go hunting and shot a young bull which we had processed and put in a locker in Cody. Again I had no idea of how to prepare it or what I was doing and had to call, once again, on dear Elly to find out different ways to cook elk. In Pennsylvania my uncles and grandfather hunted deer, but venison had never been a favorite of mine so I wondered about cooking and eating elk. But sweet and gracious Elly gave me some super recipes and we found we liked it very much. What a love she was and so patient with this young dummy from PA who didn't know too much except how to have babies!

About this time, I discovered there was another little Zeller on the way! I wasn't exactly overjoyed as I didn't know how in the world I could possibly give another baby the love and all the attention it needed. I didn't feel there were enough hours in the day now, to wash, iron (Forest Service uniform shirts had to be starched and ironed), cook, clean, play, go for walks, and nurture and love three little kids, let alone four! I immediately began to have morning sickness all day every day and that didn't help my frame of mind. In those days, birth control was kind of a joke and apparently I was especially fertile.

Karl was delighted. He agreed right away to see if he could do more to help me. He never minded changing a smelly diaper or coming home in the evening and having a playtime with the kids so I could at least get dinner for all of us in peace and quiet. At that time in our lives, I don't think Karl would have minded if we would have had ten kids. He did so love a baby and gradually I accepted the fact that there would be another baby in June, and somehow all would be "right with the world."

On a really beautiful Indian summer day I decided that the whole house needed a good cleaning and sprucing up. All three of the kids were outside playing in Skip's dirt pile, the windows were open and I felt just great. After changing sheets on the beds and both cribs, picking up clutter, sorting through and throwing out, I decided to wash all the floors. Since they were all hardwood and I had been brought up to think that a wet mop was a "dirty word," I got down on my hands and knees and washed every floor in the house, except the living room which had carpet. Then it was time to wax them all. By the time I was through, my back ached and my knees felt as though someone had hit them with a crowbar. I was just about finished and what a sense of accomplishment! I had a bucket of dirty water still sitting in the kitchen and just as I finished and was easing my aching back into a standing position, Skip came in from outside, walked into the kitchen carrying a cat one our neighbors had given to the kids, walked over to the bucket and just…dropped the cat into the bucket!

That cat gave a yowl that could be heard for miles, literally exploded out of the bucket, and soaked and dripping with dirty water was jet propelled toward the bedrooms! He went berserk and managed to distribute dirty water and footprints on every bed, dresser, and floor in the house! I was horrified, disgusted and ready to spank a little boy. Then the sight of that ridiculous cat got the better of me and I slid to the floor and laughed so hard the tears ran down my cheeks. Walt Disney would have given a million dollars for that scene! Poor Skipper was now thoroughly confused by his mother's reaction and big sad tears filled his eyes. I gave him a big hug, told him to take the kitty, who had calmed down by now, outside, wipe it dry with a rag, and never to do that again. Then I took a deep breath, got a clean bucket of water and wiped up the mess.

Fall was fast approaching and I wanted one more chance to shoot an elk before hunting season was officially over, so one morning I awoke to cold fall darkness, dressed quietly in warm clothes and made my way to the kitchen. I turned on the small light over the kitchen sink and put some water on to heat for just a quick couple of swallows of instant coffee. It was about 6 a.m. and I moved into the semi-dark living room where we had set out the rifle and my jacket, gloves and boots, the night before. I finished dressing in the dim light and headed outside, hurrying just a little bit. The kids would be waking up soon and I wanted to be gone before then. I stepped into the cold dawn air and headed for the car, started it and drove quietly and slowly up the hill and down the guard station lane to the main road. Karl would get the kids up and ready for the day. I would be back by mid-morning at the latest. Karl suggested a game trail down the road several miles that had fresh tracks from recent elk and I headed in that direction.

The dim early morning light gave yet another dimension to that incredible country. All was quiet and calm, with no hint of a breeze or the activity that would come with sunrise. The unceasing and relentless struggle of all living things in those eternal hills to survive, was a constant. The humans who lived there were not immune either. Food, shelter, and clothing were as necessary to us as to the animals and nature would dictate who would survive and who would die. Several miles down the road I found the trail, which was fairly wide and obvious, even from the car. I pulled off to the side, parked, retrieved the rifle and shells from the back seat, loaded the gun, put the safety on, and was ready to go. I immediately felt the anticipation and excitement. Wouldn't it be great if I did actually shoot an elk? What a story I would have, not only for Karl, who would be proud of me, but for my folks and his, in Pennsylvania.

Into the woods I went, among the big old spruce and fir and rocks and moss. It was getting much lighter and I could see some distance ahead. A squirrel scolded me from high on a branch and informed me I better let his winter cache of cones alone! Nature's world was awake and I was ready and watchful. It was so easy to forget why I was there and I daydreamed along the way, considering how lucky I was to be in this place. I remembered how tearfully I said goodbye to all those people I loved in Pennsylvania and were so dear to me. I had been close to sobbing when the goodbyes were said as we didn't know how much time would go by before we would see any of them again. Then Aunt Claire came up to me and said, "Joanie, this is the chance of a lifetime for you to get out of here and make a new life in a whole new world. Be happy and take it!" There were many times throughout my life that I remembered those words.

Suddenly I caught a glimpse of something big and dark moving through the trees and underbrush way ahead of me. It wasn't an elk but I wasn't sure what. I stopped, focused, held my breath, and emerging from the trees, came a huge bear! Naked hysterical panic took over! I couldn't think or breathe or move! Pure terror engulfed me and totally absorbed my whole being. I stood there trying to sort out what I was seeing with what I was supposed to be doing. I was facing the "highest rung on the food chain" and I COULD NOT FUNCTION! He (or she) moved first. He faced me and then stood up on his hind legs with paws in the air and nose in the air, and began to swing his head back and forth. He was trying to decide who and what I was and presumably, whether I was worth coming after for a mid-morning snack! It was enough to break the grip of pure naked terror. I finally remembered that I had a very powerful rifle in my hands. I couldn't remember at first how to take the safety off, and it was a remarkable feat, considering how hard I was shaking. But my brain was saying, "You have to make some decisions, dummy, or you could die!" I raised the rifle and sighted on that bear determined that I wasn't going to start anything, but if he did, I would finish it, IF I could just get the damn gun to stop shaking! Right then, I wasn't sure who the executioner would be in this situation, but I hoped it wouldn't be the bear! After an eternity, he dropped down on all fours and quietly melted into the woods.

I had enough hunting to last several lifetimes and only wanted to get out of there and head for the safety of the car and home. I turned and started back down the way I had come. I was totally breathless, my adrenalin was furiously pumping and I wanted nothing so badly as to run as fast and as hard as I could! Something told me not to and I walked at a brisk pace. I was probably not a mile into the woods but it seemed as though I was on a treadmill going nowhere. I may have walked for five minutes or so and I was close to terrified tears when ahead of me, on the trail, he appeared again! I stopped, dumbfounded and unbelieving, caught in a nightmare, knowing I would not wake up! He had stalked me from behind and come round in front! Once again he went up on his hind legs, nose in the air and was trying to catch my scent and decide whether I really was a worthwhile snack. Now I was not only trembling and weak but had reached the point of "cornered rat" and again I raised the rifle and focused as best I could. I also talked to him in a loud voice and said something like, "Get out of here, you son of a bitch!" This encounter was a duplicate of the first and after some indeterminable time, he again went down on all fours and ambled into the woods. I stood there not knowing what to do but self-preservation took over and I had to somehow make it out of the woods to the road and the car.

I walked backward, forwards, in circles, afraid I would trip and fall and he would be on me in seconds. I even fired the rifle twice on that horrible hike out, hoping the noise would keep him at bay. But I never saw him again, finally reaching the car, diving inside, slamming the door and sobbing in relief. I believe to this day, he was a grizzly, but under those circumstances, any bear would have seemed huge and I was not well enough educated at that time, and too frightened, to look for the hump on the back that distinguishes grizzlies from black bears.

I collected my sanity on the way back to the ranger station and in the driveway was a car with Florida license plates. The kids were outside playing and I got my usual "Hi ,Mommy. Did you shoot an elk?" Sitting at the dining room table were two obvious hunters visiting with Karl. I was introduced and one gentleman informed me that they were just questioning my husband as to where they might go in this country to hunt bear! I amazed myself by telling them very calmly and succinctly that I had just seen one, gave them directions on how to get there and we sent them on their way. Later that evening, as I told Karl my tale, the remembered fear of the encounter with the bear returned and so did the tears but he held me close while I diluted my fears with my tears. Another memory I will have all my life and one that I now cherish.

The aspens were turning yellow, the air was crisp and cold and during those blue-sky autumn days, the sky was filled with ducks and geese winging their way south. When the kids and I made our way for a walk in the woods or a drive down the road to Swamp Lake to watch the moose, the world was filled with the sights and sounds and smells of a wilderness getting ready for winter. Jackets were the order of the day and just like the animals of the woods, Skip, Heidi and even the little guy, Chris, were full of an extra bounce and energy, as though they too could sense that it was time to get ready for whatever winter would bring! Where were we going to be and what was going to happen to us? John told us that Crandall was shut down in the winter and we would move to Sunlight around the first of October for a month or so and then we would have to spend the worst snowy months in Cody. Karl asked if we could possibly spend the winter at Sunlight, but John was adamant about me being pregnant and didn't want to take a chance on the possibility of an episode like he and Elly went through.

In the meantime, the weather continued to get cooler and the fireplace fires were just not enough to keep warm, so the furnace in the basement had to be fired up and it immediately began to consume great quantities of wood but it worked beautifully and kept us toasty warm. To bring the kids in from the cold outside, run into the hall to stand over the main big register and feel all that warmth was a real treat for the kids and Mom and Dad too. It was also an excellent dryer for wet snowsuits and boots. There have been times in my life since then that I wished it were possible to have a big main register in some hallway where I could stand in the wintertime and feel that wonderful warmth. Of course, the cutting of the wood and the hauling out of ashes was not part of my reminiscing.

Karl decided it was just too much of a temptation listening to all those flights of ducks and geese and decided to go hunting to add some fowl to the "larder." The sky was filled with "honkers" and he might even be able to bag a goose, although most of the time when they flew over, their winged v-formations were so high above us, the kids and I really had to scan the heavens to find them, although we could hear them honking and talking to each other as they flew south. Sometimes we would be actually in the house and one of the kids would look upward and say, "Mommy, I can hear the ducks, let's go look!" And we would.

Karl had done quite a bit of pheasant hunting and he proudly brought home two ducks. The kids had to help clean them, but first they wanted to hold them upside down by the feet and get their pictures taken. I heard much giggling coming from outside and when I looked toward the office, there were feathers flying everywhere and a lot of fun noises as the ducks were plucked and cleaned.

Now it was my turn to put my culinary talents together and make a memorable feast from the bounty of the forest. I was not going to ask Elly. I would do this one myself. Out came the cookbooks and I finally found a recipe for wild duck that indicated you sliced all kinds of onion, oranges, apples, etc. into the cavity of the bird, baked it and then discarded the "filling" as it would absorb the wild taste. I, oh so carefully, followed directions, seasoned the ducks and after much preparation popped them into the oven. I had the rest of the meal planned to make this a kind of miniature Thanksgiving—they were beautiful!

John happened to come by an hour or so later and we were all having a cup of coffee at the table, when an odd odor began to come from somewhere. It became stronger and very unpleasant, almost like a raw sewage smell, but I knew Chris's diaper didn't need changing and my child certainly never smelled like that! Finally, it dawned on me that it must be coming from the oven and when I opened the oven door to check, the odor was incredibly awful! I said something about the ducks and John said, "That's your problem, those are swamp ducks and they eat fish and swamp grasses and their meat absorbs the smell." Can you imagine what a "fishy" duck would taste like? Again, yet another learning experience. I felt sorry for Karl, the ducks got tossed and it was years before I could even taste duck, even though I was assured they were grain fed!

On a cool fall day, we were invited to Sunlight to watch the preparations for a week-long horseback pack trip that Karl, John, Paul McMillan, the forest supervisor, and some of the men from Denver were going to take into the high country. Horses had to be hauled to Sunlight from Crandall, panniers full of groceries had to be packed and lashed on to the backs of pack horses, saddle bags filled with personal belongings, tents loaded, sleeping bags wrapped and packed. The whole process was pretty exciting to watch.

When we got there, the corral was full of about thirty horses; some from Crandall, some from Sunlight and a few rented by the Forest Service from Ronnie. Horses who don't know each other don't get along very well and there was much milling, kicking, squealing, biting and raising dust. The horses from Sunlight had just been rounded up that morning and apparently it was quite a job to get them corralled. They were really feeling their oats! So were the guys and the atmosphere was one of happy anticipation. There was a lot of good-natured kidding and teasing as the gear was spread out and it was about time to start packing and saddling the horses.

Heidi, Skip, and Bret had climbed up on the corral gate to watch the excitement and especially the horses in the corral and all three of those little kids were about as wound up as the horses. We'll never know which one did it, but somehow, someway, the latch was lifted on the gate and it slowly swung open with three little kids hanging on to the side of the gate for dear life and thirty ornery "wild" horses made a dash for freedom! The men stopped dead in their tracks, openmouthed and disbelieving as the horses jumped the obstacles of saddles, ropes, panniers, tack, groceries, and went charging off into the meadow. Fortunately, there were some saddled horses ready to go and these were quickly mounted and off they went! After some minutes of riding hell bent for leather, amidst muttered and vocal obscenities, whistling and a lot of yelling, the rodeo ended with all the horses being chased at full gallop back into the corral. Elly and I were ready to protect our children from a "fate worse than death" but the guys were really good-natured about it and no harm done. Off they went and the kids and I drove our lonely little Chevy back to Crandall.

Sometimes it was so hard to be without Karl. The kids missed him too and would ask out of the clear blue, "When is Daddy coming home?" Of course he always did come home and some weeks later we woke to a gray, blustery, bitterly cold day. The wind whirled and nipped at the few remaining leaves on the trees, determined to disrobe them completely in preparation of the winter to come. By afternoon, there were a few obvious snowflakes intermingled with the flying leaves and dust. The phone rang one long and one short and it was John calling to tell us to pack up, we were moving to Sunlight, and he would be over with someone to move us in the morning! In that country a smattering of snowflakes could turn to a blizzard quickly and deposit several feet of snow in a matter of a few hours. He wanted us out of there, NOW!

Since the house was pretty much furnished, we really hadn't accumulated any more personal possessions in the few months we had been there. All our worldly goods had come West in a small U-Haul trailer and we were still pretty mobile. The snow had only put down a dusting overnight but the day dawned cold and raw! Karl and I had just about everything ready to go except for dismantling the cribs after we had the kids up, fed and dressed. John and his helper arrived and in a fairly short while, the kids were in their snowsuits, we were loaded, the house was winterized, and we were off to more adventures in Sunlight!

We would not be back to Crandall till winter was over, the snow was gone, and the country opened up again.

From the top of Dead Indian Hill looking West
to the mountains of Yellowstone. Photo: Joan Duncan

Swamp Lake today. Photo: Joan Duncan

Swamp Lake in 1957. Photo: Karl Zeller

The author with her memories on the porch at Crandall
in 2002. Photo: Joan Duncan

Our wilderness cowgirl with Bitsy's puppies.
Photo: Karl Zeller

Skipper and his earthworks project. Photo: Karl Zeller

Sharp and Skip with Dad's ducks and shotgun.
Photo: Karl Zeller

They just had to hold the ducks! Photo: Karl Zeller

The trusty Dodge power wagon that enabled us to go when nothing else would. Photo: Karl Zeller

The famous fence posts on top of Dead Indian Hill-1958.
Photo: Karl Zeller

Our first Christmas cookies baked in the kitchen of the bunkhouse 1958. Photo: Karl Zeller

Our family is complete! Photo: Karl Zeller

And then there were four! 1958. Photo: Karl Zeller

The author revisits Sunlight in 2002 and the bunkhouse is even smaller than remembered. Photo: Joan Duncan

Part II
Sunlight to Cody, Then Back to Crandall

From Crandall we headed down the main road toward Sunlight. John and his helper were riding in the pickup and pulling a horse trailer, both vehicles full of our worldly possessions plus precious toys. It was another new and uncommon experience to have personal possessions transported in a horse trailer. It also looked as though it had only been swept out rather quickly and I made a mental note to check our furniture for any signs of horse manure after we were unloaded. Karl drove our trusty little Chevy. Skip and Heidi were wound up like fast-action mechanical toys talking about being at Sunlight so they could play with John and Elly's two little boys. Heidi, of course, was immediately going to get to know the new "horsies" that she didn't know.

In about sixteen miles we crossed the little bridge over Sunlight Creek and reached the road that turned right, off the main road to Cody, and headed west through the Sunlight basin. Had we stayed on the main road, the climb out of the creek bed continued upward and became Dead Indian Hill. But today we headed down that very rough dirt road and followed the creek that had created this huge open valley that must have made the first ranchers who happened there, to deliver a "yahoo" that could be heard for miles, as they had found the perfect location to pioneer raising cattle. There was grass and water and no lack of wild game to supply the winter cache of dried meat. The creek was lined with willows, which was the favorite food and cover for moose. This was also the valley where our famous old gal Betty had her ranch. Some of the other permittees, whose relatives had homesteaded that country, lived here also. The valley floor was fairly level and as we traveled along the road, some of the houses and ranches were visible across the creek, tucked into a grove of trees or nestled against a meadowed hill with cattle dotting the wide-open meadows.

As we bounced our way through the valley we could see the highest peaks ahead of us dropping into Yellowstone Park, probably only seven or eight miles as the crow flies. One of the ridges to the park was called Baldy Mountain and aptly named. The whole top was completely bare of trees and twice, we were privileged to see one of the more spectacular sights in that country. In late fall after the first few snows had fallen in the highest country and Baldy was covered with white, there would appear on the mountain, a thin black wavy line that looked, with the naked eye, like someone had drawn with a pencil. Then if you stared long enough, it appeared to be moving or changing. And we were told that these were thousands of elk on the move, migrating from the Sunlight/Crandall country down into the Yellowstone/Jackson Hole country where, in those harsh

Wyoming winters, it was easier to find food and cover. With binoculars, the mass became as ants on the move, but somehow with the naked eye, it was an event more profound. Sometimes the line would last for several days or more than a week, sometimes very thin and then again thicker. One day you would look up and it would be gone and the mountain would again be void of anything. These many years later, I wonder if one can still see the elk migrate over Baldy Mountain?

The entire complex of the ranger station was located in a U-shaped canyon with the open end of the horseshoe being the road that ran in front. The ranger's house was log, big and beautiful and the occasional tourist or camper would think it was a lodge. There was a fairly large barn with corral, but we already know about the gate on that corral! There was also an office, garage, warehouse, workshop and various other utility buildings plus the bunkhouse which was located further up the hill and sat a little off by itself.

This is where we were to live for a short time and that's exactly what it was…a bunkhouse used by the summer employees, usually college students. It was designed in the shape of a T with the long arm being the open kitchen, which was needed in our case, for the dining, living room and play area. The cross arm was a very small bedroom with stacked bunk beds, a bathroom with shower, and the living room which had to be made into Karl's and my bedroom. There were two woodstoves for heat, one in the living room and the one in the kitchen that was actually a cook stove. The living room faced the meadow and had the front door to the outside. Downstairs, there was a small basement where the wash machine would go and occasionally I could hang a very few of the kids' clothes to dry. To say that it was a little on the small side for our family was the understatement of the year, but we would manage. Karl and I started to put things in order and discovered that there was not room for two cribs and the existing bunk beds in the bedroom, so Skip and Heidi got their own beds, Chris was in his crib, and Mom and Dad, whose bedroom was the living room, were relegated to bunk beds also! Karl took the top and I took the bottom. Might have been a good idea several months back, but oh well.

On past the ranger station only a few miles was one of the biggest ranches in that country, called the Berthold ranch, and owned, at the time, by the vice president of one of the three biggest car manufacturers in the world. That ranch was operated and run by Ronnie and his wife and children. Ronnie was a true man of those mountains and knew that country better than just about anyone living there at that time. He also was to help us through some dangerous and difficult situations.

Too many years have gone by to remember how long we were there that first winter. Part of the reason for the blur is that I was very sick and weak with that pregnancy. I just couldn't keep any food down, morning, noon, or night. Food would taste good, but after a little while, up it would come. I lost a lot of weight and became weaker and weaker. Getting through the day and taking care of the ones we already had was a major effort. I couldn't do much of anything except lie on that old couch, watch the kids play, heat some soup for their lunch and change the necessary diaper. Poor Karl had to work and come home to washing, cooking, cleaning, giving baths, playing games and was both Mommy and Daddy.

I was given injections, a changed diet and at almost three months pregnant, nothing seemed to work. My doctor, who was now our family physician and a wonderful caring individual, was very concerned as the medications just weren't working. I weighed about ninety-eight pounds and it was getting scary. On our next trip to the doctor, he was very blunt and to the point: "If you lose even one more pound, we are going to terminate this pregnancy! This is dangerous, you live too far away and you can't live like this!" When my brain actually registered what he was saying, it immediately sent a message to my body that said, "Shape up, we are not going to lose this baby!" Within a week, I was keeping food down, gaining strength and starting to feel just wonderful. Amazing how our bodies and minds work sometimes.

One of the incidents I remember vividly that first time at Sunlight, was lying on the couch, feeling terrible and in a semi-awake state and suddenly hearing the vacuum cleaner running. Skip had decided to help his mommy by cleaning out the woodstove. Only there happened to be a fire going and he was suctioning up the live coals into the vacuum! I grabbed the vacuum, unplugged it, took the cover off and headed for the outside. I pulled out the cloth bag, which was smoldering (no disposable bags in those days), dumped the contents on the ground and stomped out the fire. There were two pretty-good-size holes which I later repaired with pieces of material and a needle and thread. Poor Skip was really looking worried like he'd done it again, which he had. We made an agreement that he was to vacuum only the floors and the furniture and to ask me first.

Karl found a furnished apartment in Cody and before winter came in its fury and closed the road till spring, it was time to load up again and head for town. The apartment was in a basement and pretty dark and dreary, had terrible linoleum on the floor and the furniture was really tacky. We referred to ourselves as living in the "slums" but it was clean and roomy, quite a bit bigger than the bunkhouse and would do for a short time. We had Christmas there and with baking cookies, and all the packages from their grandparents and a tree and a wonderful visit from Santa Claus, we made that dumpy little apartment a very happy place.

The supervisor's office was in Cody and that winter, we got to know many of the Forest Service families who lived in Cody. R.B. and Jane Smith had five kids and one on the way also and she and I became good friends. Skip and Heidi and Chris also had some new friends to play with. For them and me, it was a lovely change. Jane was the epitome of the "super mom," involved with school, Boy Scouts, Girl Scouts, bake sales, picnics, etc. etc., but an absolutely terrible housekeeper! Her husband once wrote "clean me" in the dust on the refrigerator and Jane though it was hilariously funny—and ignored it. It certainly impressed me. She was also the gal who said, "If you're going to be in the Forest Service, you need to learn how to play bridge. It will be your entry into every town you ever move to." She proceeded to teach me and soon I was playing with the Forest Service wives' club and having a ball. They were a wonderful bunch of women. I will always be grateful to her for taking me under her wing and seeing that the kids and I were made welcome and kept busy meeting all those wonderful people and other children that first winter. We found Forest Service families, wherever we went, and all through the years, to be the same caring, fun-loving people as those first encounters in Cody.

Karl was busy from early morning on, although being in town was more like a "real job" in that he was at work by 8 a.m. and home soon after 5 in the evening. But we were more confined—no Swamp Lake to watch the moose, no walks to the cattle guard, no trips to the campground to build a fire, so sometimes the days were pretty long. There wasn't really a yard for the kids to play where it was safe, so unless we went to a park or a visit to someone else's house, they had to be inside. We got back into going to church and Sunday school and they loved to go to the stores downtown although Cody wasn't very big.

It was a good winter in many ways and with the exposure we had to other families and other children, it gave us all a good feeling about the Forest Service, their policies and the people who were part of this huge fraternity. After we left these people and went to different forests we sometimes would walk into a party and see people we had known many years before on another forest in another state! It was not uncommon to get transferred about every two years, so there were a lot of people moving around a lot of the time. With the meetings Karl had in Denver, which was the headquarters for Region II at that time, he was kept informed as to when and where some of our friends had gone.

We were busy and happy but always in the back of my mind the clock kept running, keeping track of how long before the baby was born and how long before we could get back to Crandall. I had totally given my heart to that country and couldn't wait to get back. I felt absolutely wonderful and full of energy and was getting bigger by the minute, but that didn't stop Karl and me from going to two Forest Service parties that year, one on New Year's and one on Valentine's Day. I put on my very best maternity outfit, danced, ate and we both had a super good time. Also my first introduction to a rare steak, completely unheard of in Pennsylvania Dutch country. My mother didn't consider a piece of meat "done" until it was almost burned black, which sort of resulted in a "tough as a boot" piece of meat. The first time I bit into a steak cooked rare at one of the Forest Service banquets, I thought I'd died and gone to heaven! Wow! What a treat! For Karl too! We weren't very sophisticated. This whole lifestyle was new and exciting and we both found we loved to dance!

The air was getting warmer, snow was melting and the first whiffs of spring were definitely in the air. Easter had come and gone and it was getting close! About this time Karl came home one evening and said, "The road's open. How would you like to go back to Crandall? Tomorrow?!" Yes, Yes, Yes!!

We left Cody on a beautiful spring day and still had to gun the engine of the little green Chevy and take a run at patches of snow and big muddy places in the road. The mud flew everywhere, which had Skip and Heidi and Chris convulsed in laughter and I wondered how our few pieces of furniture and cribs were faring in the open horse trailer, but I didn't care. I could clean them when we got there! As we climbed to the top of Dead Indian Hill, it was obvious that Old Man Winter hadn't been gone for very long. There were still huge patches of snow everywhere and the view to the west showed the mountains in Yellowstone to be solid white. But where the snow was retreating, there were tiny little blades of green just starting to come up. Now we were home and it was wonderful to be out of the "slums" and back in the wilds again. The kids immediately wanted to "go out and play, please, please can we, please??!!" You bet, and I went with them.

I had a doctor appointment for a check-up about a week later and he told me he thought the baby would be born about the middle of June. He also told me I had developed a heart murmur. He felt that it was only a functional murmur and would leave as soon as the baby was born and didn't really feel that it was much of a problem at all. When he put a date on the birth, we talked to our folks in PA and Mom and Pap Zeller said they would come be with us to help and to see their newest grandchild. They would come about the tenth of June. My mother, sister and Jesse would come when Mom and Pap left. Since Mom Z had never been to Crandall, we were excited about showing it to her as we knew she loved and appreciated the beauty of the outdoors too. Since this was number four and my other deliveries had been short and sweet, none of us, including the doctor, felt that I would be able to make it in time from Crandall to Cody if labor started there. And heaven only knew what the road would be like when the time came, especially if it had just rained.

We were wondering what the best solution to this problem would be when Robert and Ellen Means from Cody very graciously offered to have me stay with them until the baby was born. Robert was also in the Forest Service and worked in the supervisor's office. He and Ellen had three children of their own and the whole family, including the kids, was very caring. They insisted they had an extra bedroom, but I often wondered later if two of the kids had to double up while I was there. It would be a relaxing and happy time waiting for the baby to decide to make its appearance and maybe I could be of some help in their home.

When Pap and Mom came, it was so much fun with lots of hugs and kisses and excited kids. But in a few days I had to leave and go to Cody and when the time came, I couldn't swallow and I couldn't talk. I held the three I already had tight in my arms and it was so hard to let go. Chris was just nineteen months old and though I knew they were in excellent hands, it was so heart-rending to walk out the door without them. But I had to go and on June 14, 1958, Eric Paul Zeller came into the world in the Cody hospital and on that day, in that year, it was not only Flag Day, but it was also Father's Day! Dr. Stelter was elated with the job he and I did, as natural birth was just coming into being and we pretty much did it with only a "little bit" of pain numbing help. Karl was so proud and so happy and Pap and Mom came the next day too to welcome another grandchild and give me a hug for a "job well done."

Now I couldn't wait to get out of there and back to Crandall but that wasn't to be for a long time. The doctor told me that the heart murmur was still present and he didn't think if was a very good idea to go back to Crandall to that higher elevation. He was still confident that it would leave as I recovered from the birthing process and got my strength back. The Means family was generous again and offered their home and the spare bedroom to me and the newborn. I wasn't supposed to lift anything, not even Eric. To feed him, Ellen would get him and carry him to me with the formula and the bottle all ready to go. What a love she was! I can never repay what she and her family did. Diapers and my own clothes were washed, baby bottles were sterilized, formula was made, I was fed and I couldn't lift a finger to help. At the end of the first week I went back to the doctor and found out that yes, it was still there and, No, I couldn't go back home just yet.

This went on for about three weeks and I was so discouraged and lonely. It was doubly frustrating as I knew I had to be putting a strain and burden on the Means, although they never showed any impatience and were always so kind and pleasant. At one point, Karl came to town with Mom and Pap and the three kids for a visit, but it was too hard to see them leave without me and the tears flowed for a long time after they left. It was truly consoling and a blessing to have our newest baby, who was yet another and perfect miracle, and I tried to tell myself to be thankful and patient but it was so difficult! I was getting very depressed.

But finally, I was OK and could go home! Eric was such a good baby and it was nice in some ways to have him all to myself for a while without worrying about the other three. When Karl finally came for us and loaded the car with all the baby paraphernalia and we headed for Crandall, I talked to Eric all the way home and told him what a fun place it was and what wonderful brothers and a sister and grandparents he had.

When we got there it was early afternoon and Chris was taking a nap. Mom had done a tremendous job of keeping everything in a normal routine with three little children that she really wasn't used to caring for anymore. She looked a little weary but not too much so, and I'm sure Pap helped, at least with Skip and Heidi. I gave Skip and Heidi their loves and hugs and held them tight and put Eric in his crib which Mom had all comfy and ready to go. Then I listened to Heidi and Skip tell their tales of all the exciting and fun happenings while I was gone while we waited for Chris to wake up from his nap. When he did, Mom brought him from his crib and I started to cry because I was so happy to see "my baby." Well, that was the wrong thing to do as he buried his head in Mom Z's neck and wouldn't have anything to do with me for several days! But I understood. I had to work up to being his mother again and he made me "pay" for leaving him alone for so long. But eventually it all came together and I was able to hold him and love him like I always had.

One of the stories Mom Z told of her adventures with the kids while I was gone, was that one day she suddenly missed Heidi and couldn't find her anywhere. She called and no answer and looked everywhere. Pap was with Skip and Chris, so Mom headed down toward the warehouse. As she got closer, she noticed a lot of commotion coming from the horse corral. All twelve or so horses were in that small corral as they were being readied for a pack trip. In the middle of that milling, kicking and biting mayhem was three-year-old Heidi, smiling and admiring her favorite creatures! Mom didn't know what to do and called to her and she just walked to the fence and Mom was able to scoop her up and out of there. Then she scolded Heidi pretty severely for doing that and scaring her grandmother half to death. Back to the house they went and all this had to be related to Pap, who also gave a rather stern lecture to Heidi about horses and how they could hurt her. She listened and then went to Mom Z and beckoned for her to lean down, which Mom did, and Heidi whispered into her ear, "When are you going home?"

Eventually it was time for them to go and what a sad parting it was. Having them be our family and with us for such a long time was truly special. What remarkable loving people they were, and so patient and kind and fun with the kids. What a fine parent example for me to follow, if I could. But we would see them maybe next spring as we thought by then, we would want to go to PA for a visit if we could work it out.

A few days later, we went to Billings, Montana, and picked up my mother, sister Kathy, and brother Jesse at the train station. This necessitated going over one of the most spectacular passes in the United States. Bear Tooth Pass to Red Lodge, Montana, and then on to Billings, is an absolutely beautiful trip and very rugged although it is a two-lane paved highway. Even forty-five years later, that pass is closed from October 15 until the snows melt in the spring.

My mother would continue the job of helping me with the new baby and the other three. She always was the supreme organizer and Mrs. Clean! So the house got dusted, mopped, and polished, inside and out, everything that wasn't nailed down got washed and if it was nailed down, it got scrubbed anyway, ironing was done, and everything was PUT IN ORDER!

She did so love the kids too and one day she heard that

Bambi was at the drive-in movie theater in Cody, and could she and Karl take Kathy, Jesse, Skip and Heidi to see it? I would stay home with Chris and Eric. It meant that the movie-goers wouldn't be home till one or two in the morning, but the kids could sleep and it would be OK for just this one time and what a treat it would be! Hot dogs, popcorn, soda pop and the whole bit! I fed and bathed the two I had and put them to bed and decided there was no point in staying up so I went on to bed and to sleep.

About 3:30 Eric woke up and I fed him a bottle, but no sign of Karl and Gram. I was wide awake by then and getting really concerned even though I knew the road was in as good a shape as it could be. Finally around 4:30 I heard the car. Everybody was fine but when they got halfway up Dead Indian Hill on the way home, the generator started to act up and the car's headlights wouldn't stay on. Karl couldn't see so Mother leaned out the window and held a flashlight on the road. At least Karl could drive but it was a very long slow way! The adults were exhausted but the next day the kids, who slept most of the way, raved about the fun they had, and *Bambi* was the topic of conversation for quite a while.

We didn't have extra beds or an extra room, so while they were with us, they slept on the floor on quilts, pillows and sleeping bags borrowed from the Forest Service. Skip and Heidi thought that was great, so some nights they joined them. One night we were awakened to sudden screaming and yelling and discovered Kathy, who was about fourteen years old, in hysterics, jumping up and down. When we finally calmed her down, something had run over her bare back while she was sleeping and of course, it had to be a mouse. Everybody was awake and suddenly Jesse, who was about seven years old, yelled, "There it goes!" The mouse headed for the kitchen and

Karl grabbed a broom and whacked it dead, at which point, Skip yelled, "There goes another one!" and sure enough we saw it scamper into the vent at the bottom of the rock fireplace. There was no way to get at it in there, so Karl said he'd put books in front of it and make a barricade so it couldn't get out into the living room. That made Mother and Kathy feel secure and everyone settled down for the rest of the night.

The next day it was discovered that the vent was open clear around the back of the firebox and all the mouse had to do was run around the back and come out the other side! My mother wasn't too happy about spending the night in a mouse habitat but we set traps everywhere and finally caught the other one. They were just little deer mice and really pretty little critters, but a mouse was a mouse to my mother and she didn't like them dead or alive!

While my family was there, we had a fun time mostly being together, caring for the new baby, taking walks with the kids down to the cattle guard and back, watching the moose, going to the dump and watching the bears. Kathy, who also loved horses, got to take a few rides on a Forest Service horse and one time was caught in a summer shower and came home soaked to the skin, which she thought was the greatest thing that ever happened. She loved horses almost as much as Heidi. We went to Cooke City for an ice cream and strolled the streets of that old Western town and the whole visit was a lovely family time together. Skip reluctantly allowed Jesse to play in his dirt pile although he really didn't want to. Skip was four and a half and Jesse was seven, and those two didn't get along very well, so Mother and I had to do some refereeing. After one of their "battles" Mother gave them a talking-to about being family and didn't Skip realize that Jesse was his uncle and they should love one another. Skip replied, "I'm not calling that kid, uncle!" And he didn't. Those two always did had a tough time getting along until they were well into their teens.

Having my mother with me was a much-needed boost to my morale and self-confidence. She guided me into the transition of taking care of four little children instead of three, which I had been so concerned about before Eric was born. She helped me establish a routine that worked and I knew I would be fine. But the time passed so quickly and then, it was time for them to leave also. We drove the three of them back to the train in Billings for their journey home to Pennsylvania. How can you possibly thank someone you love so much for being such a great mom? She was always so cheerful and positive about everything and no chore was too hard or too much trouble. Again, it was so terribly hard to say goodbye and we all waved with tears in our eyes as the train slowly pulled out of the station. To cheer the kids and me (and I think Karl too), we went to a lovely little restaurant and had lunch before we headed back to Crandall. For the kids, to eat out was always such a treat and they were always on their very best behavior when we did.

With all the great caring help I had, I now was healthy and strong and full of energy and eager to get back to being the Mom in charge of our home. And now we had four! Eric fit right into our routine and it wasn't very much more for me. Now we were just us, as a family again, and continued with our routines. Karl on occasion would go to Cody for groceries and take Skip with him, leaving me at home with the three smaller ones. It was easier than packing everyone up to go to town, and it always was such a long, tiresome day. So Heidi and I stayed home and took care of the little guys. We had been promised a treat if we were good and when Daddy and Skipper finally showed up with our two weeks' supply of groceries, they had a new record for the kids to listen to: *The Ugly Duckling*, which they loved but they called it "Huckly Duckly."

One day about mid morning I heard much giggling and squeals and Skip's hearty laughter coming from out back. I finished changing Eric, put him in his playpen and went to see what was going on. Chris was now about a year and a half old and I would permit him outside with Skip and Heidi occasionally when all were admonished to stay close to the house or play in Skip's dirt pile. So the three of them were out there and as I opened the back door, I beheld three little children in different awkward positions, all trying to get their arms around and their faces buried in this huge black dog! His tail was wagging furiously and he was licking faces and trying to get closer to them just as they were to him.

He looked like a Lab but was way too big for the breed and also had a white spot on his chest which indicated some other parentage besides Lab. Where had he come from? Whose dog was he? He greeted me with the same undisguised affection and pushed his big bulk against my legs to avail himself for the petting, rubbing and hugging which was sure to come. Resistance to that kind of a greeting was impossible and I found myself hugging and petting also. Maybe his owner was down at the work center or perhaps a tourist had lost him. He had no collar and no tags, but was obviously well fed and a magnificent and beautiful dog. He obviously adored the kids and any fears I might have had about this mammoth were dispelled when I observed, even with his huge bulk, how he stepped carefully around them, although his tail was quite impossible to control and they got a few good whacks from the furious and happy wags. They pushed him down on the grass and all three crawled all over him, wrestling, laughing and having a good romp.

It had been so sad when we moved to Sunlight and then to

Cody and Bitsy had to be given away to a rancher at Sunlight who had grandchildren who would give her a lot of love. So the kids were without a dog and lavished all their saved-up attention on this black stranger who had just shown up out of nowhere. He stayed for several hours and finally I had to call the kids in for a late lunch. When they went back outside he was gone. We talked about our visitor and what fun he was and Skip and Heidi both said they hoped he would come back for another visit.

That evening they told their dad about the fun with the dog, but he didn't know of him or hadn't heard about a missing dog. So we put him out of our thoughts. But a few days later, he was back! This time he seemed to want to stay and lay on the porch when the kids were down for their naps and the tail would go crazy when they headed out to play with him. I didn't want to feed him or encourage him to stay as we felt he must belong to someone in that country. Sometimes he would stay for several days and even when the weather was miserable he would lie on the porch on the cold concrete and wait patiently for the kids to come out. He would leave but later be back to hobnob with the kids. I found myself looking forward to his visits.

Karl discovered he did belong to a rancher who lived about three miles away and had been a permanent resident in this country all his life. The owner related some pretty amazing stories to Karl about this dog who retrieved sticks from the Clarks Fork River during the raging spring runoff when the water was full of chunks of ice. He fearlessly treed bears whenever he found one, and had a healed bullet crease on his skull from a hunter who caught him stealing his cache of meat hanging on a tree about eight feet up! His owner told us that he knew the dog had been missing more than usual and if it meant that much to the dog to be with our kids, we could just keep him! His name was Sharp and after we got to really know him, we suspected that his owner was content to get rid of an unruly wild nuisance, which he was. This was a domestic animal who grew up with very little training and for the most part, was allowed to run wild and come and go as he pleased.

Karl tells the story of taking this huge dog on a particular pickup truck/ horseback ride one time and Sharp jumping into the back of the pickup, which already had been loaded with Snip the horse, who didn't think too much of sharing the truck with this dog. So Sharp reluctantly rode in the cab with Karl. After the horse was unloaded and saddled, they headed up Crandall Creek with Sharp scouting ahead, chasing all manner of wildlife, including rabbits, chipmunks or anything that moved, covering great distances in the process. He couldn't do anything without howling or barking but suddenly the bark changed to a note of extreme urgency and when the trail came abreast of the commotion, Karl dismounted to go see what it was all about. Sharp was at the base of a tree, raising ol' billy hell and looking up. When Karl followed suit, there was a terrified black bear about twenty feet up, clutching branches for all he was worth!

He was also a dog who could swim in a fast-moving river and bark at the same time. I need to relate one more story that Karl loved to tell about this dog. This happened after we were transferred to Meeker and Sharp went with us. From the Lost Creek ranger station, Karl, the ranger, and another fellow made a walking trip up the South Fork Trail to read big game browse transects. Sharp was again ranging at least a half mile ahead and very noisy as usual, when the barking suddenly changed again to that "I've got a bear treed" sound. They hurried toward the noise and found Sharp in the middle of the river, barking, howling, swimming, and herding an utterly distraught ewe to the left bank where he had already driven not only an 800-head band of ewes and lambs, but also a thoroughly unnerved herder and his horse as well. Sharp was persuaded to return to Karl while most sincere apologies were offered to the herder.

In the meantime though, he became our dog and all of us loved him to pieces although he could be a rogue and a pirate on occasion. He was almost as wild as the inhabitants of the forest and was never really tamed. He allowed us to feed him and love him only up to a point, then he was his own "top dog." He couldn't tolerate a collar and refused to be tied so there was a constant threat of him being shot by some rancher for an infraction of the rules, such as chasing sheep or cattle, but that possibility was the price of his freedom. He really wasn't the ideal pet for a forest ranger who was supposed to assume the role of both a domestic and wild animal protector. When Sharp was in the house he was well mannered but one always had the feeling that he just wasn't totally comfortable inside, even in the coldest weather.

Now we were into August and because of the head start I received from the folks, I was able to keep our routine going and we again began to take our little excursions to Swamp Lake and down to the cattle guard. The weather was so delightful with deep blue skies, enormous white clouds, warm temperatures and only an occasional rain. It felt so invigorating to be out and exploring with my little adventurers again. To look through the eyes of a child and appreciate the shape and color of a rock or a twisted and tortured stick from a tree, or a bug crawling into a hole, opens up a whole new world for a parent and I would always treasure what they taught me to see.

The phone rang one morning and it was my Uncle Charlie calling from Cody to tell me that he and my Aunt Ethel and my grandfather, Pop, had made the trip from Pennsylvania and were coming to see us! It was a great surprise but we had had several days of hard rain and I knew they wouldn't be able to negotiate Dead Indian Hill without chains or some help. As luck would have it, Karl was in Cody at the supervisor's office. He had gone in that morning. I called him and he was able to meet with our guests and talk about how to get to Crandall. My uncle drove an older but well-maintained Buick sedan and prided himself on being able to drive in any conditions—he was the hardworking dairy farmer—but Karl finally persuaded him and my Aunt Ethel that it would be pretty foolhardy to attempt the drive under the present conditions and could even be dangerous. The safest and best way was to travel into Yellowstone Park, the east entrance from Cody, and take the most direct loop up to the northeast entrance and exit there from Silvergate to Cooke City and then down our road off the Red Lodge Highway and from that intersection, it was only about seven miles of fairly level going. They would have to travel 140 miles versus 54 miles from Cody, but they actually would most likely get to Crandall within an hour of Karl and Pop and depending on conditions, could even get here first!

My grandfather was very young for his almost eighty years, and he had elected to come home with Karl and wanted to see for himself what this "terrible road was really like and was it really that bad?" So they got the groceries that I now needed for extra mouths to feed, and then came on. Pop later said that in some places he hung on for dear life because you had to take a run at the deeper puddles and gun the engine all the way through, with the vehicle sliding this way and that, all the time sending a prayer heavenward that you would make it. Really old-hat stuff to Karl and me, but he was so delighted and thrilled with that muddy, miserable, slow ride through the wilds to Crandall. He also thought it was truly wonderful country and very beautiful, but so empty of people.

Aunt Ethel and Uncle Charlie arrived in time for supper and had a great time with the kids and admired our new Zeller, who was now two months old and growing. Eric would charm everyone with his smile, even at two months. But the other kids loved company and had to "show" their bedroom and their toys and play games and sing songs. A fun time. The next day the road was drying out and we took them all for a ride to Sunlight and to see our usual moose, bears and ducks. Since they were on the elderly side, we gave Ethel and Charlie our bed and Pop slept on the couch and Karl and I took our turn at the super bed on the floor. The coyotes sang really close to the house that night and those three visitors thought that was pretty special.

The next evening we were sitting at the table enjoying the meal that Aunt Ethel and I put together, when suddenly Pop jumped up and yelled something like "there it goes" and took off out the front door, onto the porch, down the steps and ran like crazy across the driveway up and over the hill and out of sight! We had just caught a glimpse of something big and very brown with a huge rack—it had to be a bull moose and Pop was determined to get a better look because this guy was close and practically bumped into a corner of the porch as he went. We all rushed out to see where he went and at the top of the little hill Pop turned and headed back so we went inside and finished our meal. He came in a few minutes later just shaking his head, all out of breath, and couldn't believe what he had just seen and was so thrilled. If I could pick anyone in the world to show a moose to and have it truly be appreciated, it would be Pop. He was a very special, wonderful man and my mother and the rest of his daughters thought the world of him. My grandmother stayed home because she was a fairly big lady and with her age, traveling just wasn't very enjoyable.

The next morning we ate a leisurely breakfast and then they wanted to get on their way. This was a big sightseeing trip for them and they still had a lot of places they wanted to see. So once again we waved a fond farewell to more of our favorite relatives and told them we'd see them next summer.

So we were again back to a routine and on a lovely warm evening, Skip and Heidi rode their tricycles, Karl helped Chris along and I carried Eric, and we took a slow, lazy walk down to the cattle guard just to have a change of scenery. When we got there, Skip and Heidi started walking across the metal beams back and forth across the cattle guard, which they had done many times before when suddenly, Heidi lost her balance and fell. When she did, she threw out her hands to catch herself and they went on either side of the metal beams and she hit her head on the right side of her eye! It was a horrifying accident and she was in exquisite pain. Karl said, "Forget the trikes," and he scooped up Heidi, I picked up Chris in one arm, balanced on my hip, and Eric in the other and we headed back to the house as quickly as we could. Poor Skipper had to almost run to keep up with us and when I saw the wide-eyed terrified look on his face, I slowed down and assured him that his sister was going to be all right. Heidi was crying pathetically and was in excruciating pain.

When we finally reached the house, I held her in my lap and Karl ran for cold wet wash cloths. She had a big ugly bruise on and around her eye and the swelling was becoming worse. She was beginning to look dazed and at that point we called Dr. Stelter in Cody. Since we were so far away, he didn't feel that the ride in the vehicle would do her any good and said to keep her down and quiet with ice packs. We didn't have any ice, but we did have cold packages of meat in the freezer and we wrapped those in cloths and put them on her head. By this time she was totally out of her head, alternately crying, sleeping and talking gibberish—it was so scary but the doctor had said this could happen and do the best we could to keep her quiet and that it would pass eventually. I got the other three settled for the night and Karl and I sat up with her all night. Finally she went into a healthy sleep and I sobbed with relief but kept watch anyway for the rest of the night.

When she awoke in the morning, the pain seemed to be gone but the bruise was really dreadful. Her eye was almost swollen shut and the whole side of her face was yellow and red and purple, but it only hurt to the touch and she really seemed perfectly fine. Just for that day though, we stayed quiet and read books and colored pictures and listened to records. I kept her on the couch and made her feel very special, so she had a fun day in spite of not being able to go out. Sharp came in for a short visit and wagged his tail and licked her face and told her to get better soon. And the horses showed up for a little while so she could watch them out the window while she held her blankie in one hand and sucked her two fingers on the other.

That was probably the worst accident we had while we were there, but it was a very sharp and painful reminder of how far we were from a hospital and medical care should we have an even more serious problem. Skip had fallen the summer before on a metal bucket he was carrying and cut his arm bad enough to need some stitches but that's when I learned that butterfly bandages could work almost as well and it healed nicely. Being out where we were definitely had drawbacks when it came to serious illnesses or injuries. But for now, the good Lord and her guardian angel had watched over Heidi and we would handle as best we could, whatever was in store for us in the future.

Across Crandall Creek was a piece of private property

owned by the Bransons of Cody. They were the owners of the local oil company which was quite a large operation in and around Cody. To say that they were wealthy was an understatement. They were building a huge log home on that piece of land and also an airstrip. I'm not sure how they discovered we had four children but they did and one day they drove into the driveway at Crandall in a very elegant vehicle and introduced themselves. They explained they were building the house and it would be finished soon. In the meantime our children were exactly the same ages as their grandchildren and they would be so happy to be able to meet ours. So Skip, Heidi and Chris came running and I plucked Eric from his playpen and brought him out to visit with the others. Since the two older children were never shy with anyone, Chris, who was apt to be a little reserved, soon followed their lead, and they were all visiting happily. Mr. and Mr. Branson produced some treats that they brought for the children "if it was all right with me."

That started an occasional visit by the Bransons when they would come from Cody, to check on the progress of their summer "cabin." They were a wonderful couple, very happy, very intelligent and easy to be with, so I enjoyed their visits also. They declined to come in but were content to sit on the front porch and to visit with the children. They would ask about all of their projects, Heidi's love of horses, Skip's dirt pile, and even quiet and reserved Chris at one point ran into the house and came out carrying a favorite book, which they dutifully admired. They always brought a treat for "the children." Their grandchildren lived far away I believe, in California or Oregon, and they didn't have much opportunity to see them and so ours were an indication to them of their own grandchildren's interests and growing progress.

One day they stopped as usual, visited with the kids and then asked if we would please come to dinner in their new house which had been finished for about a month. They were really enthusiastic because their own grandchildren would be coming in several weeks and they wanted our kids to "try out" the new house just to see "if any changes had to be made for the suitability of children." I couldn't believe these people, who truly were so sweet and so sincere. I told them I needed to talk to Karl but I felt probably that it would be fine and we set a date for dinner the next week. "Oh, and would chicken and dumplings be something that the children could eat?" Mrs. Branson was so excited that we were going to come and "hoped it wasn't an imposition to ask."

The big evening arrived and I had all four of them bathed and dressed in their Sunday best and Mom and Dad looked pretty good too. We pulled up to this log mansion in our little old muddy Chevy and knocked on the door. It was opened by a butler but the Bransons were right there and greeted all of us very happily, and thanked the three older ones in turn and by name, for coming to their house. Then Mrs. Branson showed us to what they referred to as the Esther Williams bedroom, in case we wanted to "freshen up." The movie star, who they were very good friends with, had spent a week with them and was the first guest in their new summer home. It was nice to have a place I could put the kids' jackets, diapers, etc., and that bedroom was as big as our house. It was a suite and consisted of a bedroom, bathroom and sitting area and the décor was lovely.

The house was incredible, probably 7,000 or 8,000 square feet. The living room was massive with windows all around to take advantage of the outdoor views. The steps leading up to the landing, which overlooked the living room and led to all the upstairs bedrooms, were each an enormous half log polished to perfection so the grain of the wood was just beautiful. The room was furnished in rustic pine and the overstuffed chairs and couches were covered with a material that had the brand of their ranch and the Wyoming state flower, the Indian Paint Brush, done in needle point on all the pieces. The fireplace was also massive stone that rose to the roof and the huge open beams were gigantic logs, as were the walls inside and out, of all the rooms. It was done tastefully and furnished to perfection.

The kids proceeded to make themselves at home and soon they were carrying wastebaskets on their heads. "Oh please don't make them stop, it's really all right." Then Skip headed up the stairs and that was "all right" also, then Heidi climbed right behind him. When they got to the landing (with their mother bringing up the rear), they looked between the railing down to their dad, who was holding Eric, and the Bransons below. At that point it became obvious that they could slip between the uprights! I had a firm hold of both of them and decided it was time to go back downstairs. Mr. and Mrs. Branson said, "Oh dear, we must do something about that!" Mr. Branson announced in a very serious voice that he "would have the carpenters back in the morning to rebuild the whole bannister so that it was safe for children."

But now it was time to go in to dinner. The dining room was log also but very elegant and lovely. We actually had delicious chicken and dumplings served by a maid and a butler. They had a highchair for Chris and youth chairs for Skip and Heidi and I will never forget that those three little guys were on their very best behavior and didn't forget their "pleases and thank-you's." After dinner Skip asked if he could go to the bathroom and, "did he remember how to go to 'our' bedroom?" He did and headed that way. We continued to visit and then suddenly way off in the distance I could hear this voice calling, "Mommmmy, could you wipe my hiiiiiinnnnyyyyy??!!" I excused myself and took care of that little chore but the Bransons were grinning from ear to ear. This was a fun evening with wonderful people who used money for happiness. One of many of our neighbors who hated to see us go when we were transferred and who we would miss also.

A week or so later Karl was gone to another Forest Service school, the kids were in bed and asleep and I was enjoying a rare quiet and relaxing evening of some soft music and a good book. Suddenly the phone rang and it was Fred from the little house at the end of the meadow. "I've got a bear trying to get in my back door and I'm going to shoot it. Stay inside and don't come out or open your doors." Well, that was just pretty exciting! I opened a living room window so I could hear and in a few minutes I heard the loud boom of a high-powered rifle!

I immediately tore out the door and ran down the meadow in pitch blackness to see the dead bear! When I got there, Fred and one of the other guys were standing over the bear with a flashlight. When Fred saw me he got pretty angry and said, "I told you to stay in the house! What if I had only wounded it?!" It never occurred to me that he wouldn't kill it dead, I just never even considered that possibility.

Now there was a question of what to do with it. If the game warden came, he would make them skin it, gut it and cut up the meat. Fred didn't want to do that, he just wanted to dispose of the bear, so Charlie ran and got some extra manpower and they lifted a good-size black bear into the back of Fred's pickup and he took it to the dump knowing the locals wouldn't say anything.

Apparently the bear had started to nose around their tiny cabin and Fred, who was mad by this time, chased it off twice, but it kept coming back and then started to scratch at the windows. It also stood up and put its front paws on the windows and doors and started to rock back and forth like they do when they're looking for food and trying to move a log. The window was only going to be able to take so much stress without breaking. That got to be very unsettling for Fred and his wife Susie and their little girl Anita. When he opened the door and hollered, the bear moved off but came right back. Fred said it had the "stamp" of a Yellowstone bear from the way it acted and decided to dispatch it with all expediency, which he did.

Life was never dull and there was always bread to bake, the house to clean, clothes and diapers to wash (lots of those), ironing to do, formula to make, and in those days we sterilized bottles also, and some days I wondered if I would have enough energy to make it through the whole day or to settle one more squabble between Heidi and Skip or wipe one more runny nose or change a diaper again or fix another "boo-boo"… "Mommy, it really hurts, could you please put a Band-Aid on it?" I heard that many times for even the tiniest little pin prick. Band-Aids were pretty special, as were Kleenex, and both were seriously overused. A Band-Aid was needed to make even the teeniest tiny scratch "feel better" and a whole Kleenex was used for a very very small sniffle or a tiny booger. It was time to enter the cost into our budget or find another solution. We switched from Kleenex to toilet paper and got very selective about the seriousnous of a wound that needed a Band-Aid. But it wasn't nearly as much fun.

The days when I was almost caught up, and the sun shone and the sky was blue, I couldn't resist taking the time to go outside and join the kids on the swing set for a lazy warm swing, usually with Eric on my lap, or a walk back to the creek to play in the water and throw sticks, or down to the work center to see if anyone was there, or a jaunt in the car to Swamp Lake or a campground to build a fire, just lots of lazy fun things to do. I just had to be aware that the four of them were so little and I couldn't put us in jeopardy of having to walk back for any distance. Before Eric was born, I would sometimes pull Chris on the wagon and Skip and Heidi could walk and then ride if they got too tired, but with Eric, it was a different story. I could manage for a very short distance, but carrying him and pulling Chris was just too much, and if Skip and Heidi got too tired, it would develop into an impossible situation, so we couldn't go very far.

The quiet and the peace of that incredible wilderness was good for my disposition, even if the kids had a propensity for shattering the stillness with squeals of discovery or laughter, or screams, or just yelling to yell! Any wildlife in our immediate vicinity always knew where we were and how close we were. We weren't too adept at sneaking up on anything.

On one Sunday afternoon, we were invited to Sunlight to get together with John and Elly, their two little guys, the supervisor Paul McMillan and his wife and two daughters, and some of the other Forest Service families from Cody and we would have a picnic. It was really a lively boisterous affair. The horses were saddled and all of the kids got to ride, guns were brought out, there was target shooting and the food was great. While we were all visiting and having a good time, some obvious "dudes" on horses rode up from one of the neighboring ranches and visited with all of us. They had just seen some moose in the willows along the creek and were pretty excited and impressed. One of the men was particularly vocal about being envious of we, who lived in that country year round, whereas he spent most of his time in New York City. Turned out that he was THE Mr. Smith, of one of the most well-known department stores in New York City! The national moguls who either lived there part-time or visited that country were amazing! And without exception, every one of them was a really nice down-to-earth human being. Maybe Mr. Benton of the cereal company was a bit grumpy, but oh well.

It was getting chilly again and we began to talk about spending the winter at Sunlight. It would mean four little children and two adults trying to survive in that tiny little bunkhouse for about five months, and there was a better-than-average chance that at least three of those months, we would not be able to get to Cody and would truly be "snowed in"! This was something Karl really wanted to do and although I had some reservations about the size of the bunkhouse, the thought of wintering in the Sunlight Basin was pretty tempting and we agreed that Karl would help with the kids as much as he could and we would be all right. Besides, I didn't want to spend another winter in Cody.

Hunting season had arrived again and Paul McMillan, the supervisor, called Karl and asked him whether he could come out to our country and hunt elk, and did Karl want to go with him? Karl liked and respected Paul and felt he was a very knowledgeable woodsman, so it followed that he would also be someone first-rate to go hunting with.

Paul came the night before the hunt started and we naturally invited him to have dinner with us that evening. He had his sleeping bag and would bunk in the office but be bright and early for breakfast the next morning. He and Karl fixed their own breakfast and were long gone before the kids and I woke up. They would take horses and Paul knew "just where to go," which was quite a long ride from Crandall. He had a meeting in Cody the next day so had to be back and on his way with or without meat in one day. We also knew there was a Fish and Game check station where our road intersected the main highway.

I sort of expected them not too long after dark but hadn't

cooked for more than just our family as I knew Paul had to leave for Cody as soon as the horses were put away. I fed the kids, gave them their baths, read our usual nighttime book and tucked them all in. I sat at the table writing letters to the folks back home and lost track of time. By 11:00 they still weren't back but I thought that they probably had bagged an elk and had gotten farther away from Crandall than they planned. They also would have had to take care of the meat and that requires quite a bit of time. I wasn't too concerned as both Paul and Karl knew their way around in the woods and how to take care of themselves. Finally I went to bed.

I was awakened in the deep of the night by Karl getting quietly into bed with me. It was 4 a.m! He said, "I'll tell you in the morning" and I had to be satisfied with that—he obviously was all right and Paul was loaded and on his way to Cody.

The story of their adventure was also a tale of Paul McMillan and his everyday "personality" when he wasn't acting in a supervisory capacity. He and Karl rode a good part of the day into the really high country and since we didn't as yet have any snow on the ground, it was hard to pick up any kind of a trail. But Karl was excited about the new and really awesome country he saw and enjoyed the day thoroughly. About the time they decided they weren't going to have any luck, they spotted a big herd of elk over a few ridges and below where they were. They moved quickly and found an overlooking vantage point and got out the glasses to look over the herd. They were after meat, not trophy heads, and there were a lot of cows to pick from.

By this time they were both pretty excited, got mounted on the horses and headed down the ridge to intercept the herd as it moved in their direction. But the wind was wrong or there were hunters on the other side of the herd because suddenly there was ground-shaking thunder and the whole herd came directly toward them! At this point they vaulted off their horses, grabbed their guns from the scabbards and attempted to pick out an animal to shoot. Apparently the herd was running full out and Karl was apprehensive about shooting and just wounding an animal. But Paul let go and before you could blink an eye, there were three dead cows lying on the open meadow! Paul and Karl both had a license and he just "happened" to have his wife's license with him, but of course, she was back in Cody and he was out here! And there was a state Fish and Game checkpoint to go through on his way back to Cody!

Paul McMillan was never daunted by anything in his life.. He produced some burlap bags from the pack saddle on the pack horse and right there and then, he and Karl gutted, skinned, and boned three huge elk! It was doubtful that the officers at the checkpoint would want to dump the burlap bags of meat and sort through to see if the meat matched the licenses. By the time Paul and Karl were through it was pitch black and they finished by holding matches so the other could see. It was so cold their hands were freezing and gloves were no good in that bloody mess. They had a vague idea of where the Crandall Creek trailhead was but were several miles away and had to travel some pretty straight up-and-down country to get back to it. Paul just said they'd have to trust the horses to go home and to just hang on. Several times they had to ride up and down such steep slopes, they both got off and led the horses or rather they hung on to the side of the saddle and the horses led them. Finally they were back on the trail but then had to watch very carefully in the blackness for overhanging branches that could knock you off the saddle and hurt you bad if you didn't duck. It was very slow going but the horses were headed home and finally they crossed the little bridge to the corral. Our share of the meat was hanging in the warehouse/garage and would be our main source of protein that winter.

The North Wind doth blow and we shall have snow.

And what will the Zellers do then?

They'll pack up their gear with nary a tear and cheerfully head for Sunlight!

Part III
Sunlight and the End of the Wild Beginning

We started to make preparations and plan our move to Sunlight for the winter. Karl had gotten permission from Paul McMillan, the supervisor, to winter in at Sunlight. The decision was made partly on the basis that John felt there were enough reports, both fiscal and otherwise, to keep them both busy in the office. There were some major policy changes being made in Washington, D.C., that would affect the Forest Service all over the United States, but in the meantime, the regional office was collecting all kinds of data from the individual forests and rangers that would help with the whole process. This is what John and Karl would do together. By this time Karl was learning that the days of the forest rangers riding the range were almost over. Big changes were coming, and not all of them necessarily to the liking of those who lived in and loved the forests, the animals and the land.

Toward the end of October, Karl came home one evening looking very glum and announced that John and Elly were being transferred and would leave sometime in November. I couldn't believe it! We knew this could happen but it was all still so new to us, and how were we going to survive without their guidance and moral support? We had learned so much from the two of them and had truly come a long way with our wilderness learning process, but still had a long way to go. Karl still had reservations about his own competency although he had been complimented on the job he was doing, not only by John, but by Paul McMillan, who let the "head honchos" in the regional office know also. Karl and John had developed a good rapport and working relationship. It would be a tough adjustment for Karl and he thought so highly of John that it would be difficult not to compare the incoming ranger with John, who truly was an exceptional person.

As was his wife Elly. Without her to lean on, I would now be absolutely on my own. By this time though, she had given me a stockpile of resources and enough confidence in myself that I wasn't fearful of her leaving. I would miss her as a dear friend who I had come to love but I believed that now I could generate and forge solutions to problems as they arose and make my own way. She had taught me well.

Did we still want to winter at Sunlight? We weren't sure but at this point the plans had been made and we felt an obligation to proceed. We had no idea who John's replacement would be. We would try to make he and his family feel welcome and at home.

The summer help was gone, Sam Burton was down from the Clay Butte fire tower and the Red Lodge Highway was closed from now to whenever the road opened in spring. At Crandall, Karl was wrapping up some things in the office and cleaning up the warehouse/garage. The horses had been hauled to a pasture near Cody for the winter. Fred, Susie, and their little girl Anita were gone till next spring. So the Crandall guard station was empty except for the Zeller family and it was wonderful! When the kids and I took our walks, the air was cold, the sun was that pale light that precludes winter, the trees were bare and the whole world was waiting to be put to sleep by snow. The feeling was one of being the only people that existed in the world with all that magnificent beauty just for us.

But it was time, and we needed to get to Sunlight soon so we could move in, get adjusted and organized, figure out where we would put all the beds we needed. Again we loaded all our treasures into our favorite moving van, which still happened to be a horse trailer. Only I had some time now to make sure it was at least swept and cleaned somewhat. This time the kids, especially Skip and Heidi, were more aware of what was going on and pleaded, "Please, can't we just stay here?" If only they knew how much I wished we could. Finally, we were ready to go and Karl drove the Forest Service pickup pulling the horse trailer and I drove our car.

We were now six, and two of the Zellers had to sleep in cribs. By some finite calculations, the two cribs and one set of bunk beds were fitted into the small bedroom but it would be quite a job to change bedding when the time came and we kind of had to step sideways into the bathroom. The kitchen was our living area as it had been before, but since we were going to be there for quite a while, we took an easy chair, end table and lamp from Crandall and set those up in one corner as a kind of living room. We certainly were cozy but we weren't quite stepping on each other when we moved about. However, there would be times when the walls seemed to converge and the margin of space became so small I would have a problem catching my breath.

John and Elly were getting ready for their move. After we got there, John and Karl were in the office all day every day and since John would be gone when the new ranger got there, it would be up to Karl to familiarize the new ranger with the Clarks Fork District of the Shoshone National Forest... A big job!. That's how the Forest Service did it. You were moved to another forest without knowing anything about it, and it was up to whoever was there to tell the incoming ranger where everything was, including the roads, campgrounds, housing, office, who the permittees were and how easy they were to get along with, who grazed cattle and who grazed sheep, how many summer employees there were, what trails went where, etc. etc. etc.!

The one person who was invaluable to the incoming rangers was the general district assistant. These were the guys hired by the Forest Service who, for the most part, were born and raised in that country and were, in their own right, the caretakers of the woods. Few had ever been to college but these were the men who had been raised with the accumulated knowledge of their years of living in that country. They knew the land, the water, the trees, the animals, and were topped off with a common-sense approach to the handling of horses, guns and the people who had been their family's neighbors long before the Forest Service arrived in that country. I don't believe its an exaggeration to say that these men where the silent backbone of the Forest Service and sadly, were never given the credit they deserved for the job they did.

So while John and Karl were making preparations for the transition, I helped Elly, mostly by keeping their two boys with our kids so she could concentrate on what she had to do. Now we started a new routine and had a different way to go to take our walks and little Bret and Michael went with us, and the way of the wilds followed us over there also.

The ranger station complex was in a canyon and we didn't have access to campgrounds, or a stream or ponds and it was just too far to get to them. For now we roamed the sagebrush, pinon, juniper, pine country that surrounded us, and now our excursions and explorations took a different bent. We searched for interesting rocks and stones and oddly shaped sticks, an occasional pretty leaf, and lots of scary bugs. When our meanderings caused a rabbit to explode out of a patch of brush it was a big thrill! When Skip and Heidi and Brett found a pile of animal scat I would try to explain how we could tell which animal made the deposit. But they always got silly and giggly and said, "Oh Mommy, you're talking about animal poop!" The nature lectures from me weren't nearly as much fun as taking sticks and batting the poop amid much giggling, and of course, the three little ones had a good time also. I missed the Crandall country much more than they did. We were to discover very soon though, that our adventures would continue even at Sunlight.

There was a full moon one night and John rang us on the telephone quite late and told us to look outside. We grabbed a jacket and softly stepped outside. The moon lit up the bushes and grass like it was day, even casting silvery shadows. John's huge yellow Lab, Sooner, was in the meadow playing with another dog. Only it wasn't a dog, it was a coyote and it was a female in heat. In a huge ring around the two of them was a band of about twelve to fifteen other coyotes in a perfect circle, spaced evenly. As we watched, it became obvious that she was a decoy sent to get Sooner interested in her while the circle slowly closed in, at which point the pack would pounce, kill the Lab and have a feast! It was incredible to watch. The female would roll on her back with paws in the air, she would crawl on her belly, rub herself against Sooner and as he got more and more interested, the circle began to move in from the edges. We knew John and Elly were watching down below us from their house, but why didn't John call his dog? The pack was closing in and Sooner was going to get killed! Suddenly there was a gunshot and the coyotes disappeared into thin air as though they had never been there. John had just fired into the air. He told us the ranchers in that country have a hard time keeping dogs for that very reason and no one had cats. It was amazing.

Chris woke up one morning several days later with a really terrible cold, crying and just miserable. He was running a pretty high fever and needed to go to the doctor in Cody. It had been raining for several days and the road was a mess, so Karl would take him in the old Dodge power wagon which had chains on all four tires. The rest of us would stay home. The phone line was working and I was able to talk to the doctor, who wanted him brought in because it sounded like a bad ear infection to him. So Karl bundled our little guy up and I sent some juice and crackers and his "blankie" plus a stuffed toy and some books. He was almost two years old—would be in about a week—and was a really sweet little boy. He did manage to get a lot of colds though and my mother always said that Chris looked like he needed a "care package." He ate well but never seemed to put on weight. No car seats in those days, so we put a blanket and pillow on the seat so he could lie down if he wanted to. He was really sick and I was concerned. They took off by the middle of the morning and we knew that getting over Dead Indian hill was not impossible but Karl would have to go very slowly and cautiously.

There were a few things that would be picked up at the grocery store for us, and John and Elly, and then they would head right home. If they saw the doctor right after lunch, they would be home by no later than six even with the road in bad shape. But when it got to be about 6:30, I rang John and he said the road was probably pretty bad and Karl was probably just taking his time, but if he didn't show up within an hour, he would go looking. We were now into November and it was pitch black outside. It was always possible to encounter an unexpected mishap in that country, even when the weather and the road were good. I knew that Karl could handle pretty much whatever came along, but a mishap of whatever kind plus a sick two-year-old could be disastrous.

Karl and Chris came in about 7 p.m. and the look on Karl's face told me the trip had not been uneventful. They saw the doctor just fine, who diagnosed an ear infection and gave Chris a prescription for some antibiotics. Karl got the prescription filled and picked up the few groceries we all needed and headed back. It was really nasty driving but all went smoothly even up and over Dead Indian Hill. However, on the road into the Sunlight basin, the road runs through a little patch of woods that seems to hold the moisture even when the rest of the road is dry. Well, by this time it was pitch black, Chris was asleep and they were within six miles of being home when Karl hit a puddle of water covering mud that was like glassy ice. They slid off the road into a swampy area and the power wagon was buried too deep to get it out under its own power. He had a sick little boy sound asleep on the seat and he had to get help. What to do?

He knew there was a phone climbing pole not too awfully far from the truck so he prayed that Chris wouldn't wake up and took the climbers and the linemen's belt for the telephone pole and stepped into the blackness, locking Chris in the truck. He couldn't see anything and the flashlight was all but useless in that black void. The mud collected on his boots till they were huge and heavy and he couldn't keep his footing on that greasy mess. With every step he slid and actually went down once or twice. He felt like he was enduring some kind of a nightmare, on a treadmill going nowhere, and his thoughts constantly returned to the sick little boy in the truck and what if he woke up!

After a frightful length of time, he reached the pole that he could climb. With his climbers and the tools, he could tap into the phone line. He called our famous Ronnie, who was one of the few that had another vehicle that would go in that country. Ronnie was on his way and Karl had to then repeat the nightmare of walking through that muck to get back to the truck and Chris. When he got there, Chris was still sound asleep and Karl said a thankful prayer. When Ronnie came, they just left the power wagon and he brought Karl and Chris the rest of the way. Another adventure that we hoped we'd never have to repeat.

Now it was time for John and Elly to leave and for us, it was a throat-catching goodbye to two people who taught us what we needed to know to live, persevere and love that lifestyle and gave us a foundation for our future no matter where we would go. Even their parting words were of encouragement and praise for the job we were doing. Together they took two tenderfoot rookies and gave us all we needed to survive whatever life's future held and wherever we would be. We would be forever grateful to whatever fortuitous quirk of fate placed us in their care for the beginning of our wild journey. A simple thank you wasn't enough but that's all we had to give them.

Several days later, the new ranger and his wife and their little girl arrived. Their names were Ed and Patty and the little girl was Julie. I suppose it was better that they were totally different than John and Elly. Patty was the original "farmer's wife" to whom box cake was a dirty word and if you don't believe me, just ask her, she'll tell you! I got told that floor mops were only for lazy people, she put up a thousand million jars of fruit and vegetables and they butchered their own game and maybe the people in this valley could learn a few things! Yup, that's what she said! Ed had his own ideas of how the Forest Service should be run and the whole world would be better off if they'd just do it his way!

Their little girl was really sweet and she loved to come up to the bunkhouse. Our four rowdy kids, so busy and noisy, kind of intimidated her though, and she would knock very quietly on the side door into the kitchen. When we opened it and she came in, she would just lean up against the door and watch the activity. She literally was fascinated by all the action going on and of course, it was all going on in one room! Since she was the only child in her family it took a little while for her to join in and play. She was about Skip's age but a very quiet four-and-a-half-year-old. Her mom and dad were nice enough and their hearts were good but both of them knew the world would be a better place if everybody just knuckled down and did things their way! Sometimes, it got a little old.

Old Man Winter was definitely on the way. We had had some light snowfalls that didn't last too long but the sky was turning that sincere "you better watch out, you're going to get it one of these days" dark look. So Karl and I put together a list of absolutely everything we thought we would need for the coming days when we would not be able to get out of the Sunlight Basin. The list had to be complete because there would be no going back for something we forgot.

At first I didn't know where to begin but gradually I learned to mentally make a menu and write down everything I would need to make ninety big meals, ninety lunches, and ninety breakfasts. Then there was the baby food Eric needed, plus how many loaves of bread is that, and how much flour do I need to make it, and what about ingredients for Christmas cookies and maybe a pumpkin pie and Karl's and my coffee and don't forget the cigarettes! Oh yes, we both smoked. So many cases of canned vegetables, canned fruits, juices, packages of yeast, sugar, shortening, powdered milk, canned milk, powdered eggs, dried fruits, and just a little amount of candy for a treat now and then, and don't forget peanut butter and jelly, and cheese that would keep, and on and on and ON! Everything from shoelaces to extra socks for the kids, to writing paper and stamps, to toothpaste, cleaning supplies, soaps for dishes, laundry and people, shampoo, and then, what if the kids got really sick?

This required a trip to see good ol' Dr. Stelter, who actually was probably about forty years old. When I related to him that we were about to embark on a three-month isolation in the wilds with four little kids, he just shook his head and grinned at our "grit." He gave me several bottles of unmixed penicillin, cough syrup, medicine for diarrhea, vomiting, headaches, toothaches and whatever else he could possibly think of and he would be available to talk to me on the phone as he wasn't going anywhere that winter. I could call him at his office or at home anytime. He was very definite about that. So I had an ace in the hole that gave me some extra confidence about having four tiny little kids out in the middle of nowhere.

When we actually went to the grocery store and purchased all that we needed, the tape seemed to be miles long and the figure was astronomical even for that time. The clerks took it all in stride though as we were not the only people in that country surrounding Cody who needed to get ready for the winter that always came, and when it did, halted all traffic commuting between the outlying areas and Cody. The power wagon was loaded and it was almost full, the kids were wide eyed with wonder at all the groceries—"Are we going to eat all that?!"— and we headed for home. It took many hours to put things in their places and to check the list again and again to make sure we had everything. When it was finally done though, we had a smug contented feeling that winter could come, we were ready, and could face anything she could throw at us! Would we ever learn not to be overconfident?

It had been freezing every night for over a month and our elk was still frozen solid in the bag that Paul McMillan had put it in, blood, hair and all. It was literally a burlap bag full of frozen meat in one huge lump. Later when we were snowed in, Karl would go out, peel back the bag, take a saw and saw off what we thought was enough for a meal, stew, or whatever I wanted to fix. I know we roasted steaks and stewed roasts and chicken-fried stewing meat, but oh well, it was meat. I had to thaw it and wash it each time. Finally by the time March arrived and there wasn't a whole lot left, when I got it to the table, I could eat and enjoy it, but the smell of that wild meat cooking got to be almost more than I could bear and I was not even pregnant! We also had some hams, hamburger and a little pork that was either canned or frozen and stored, but elk was our mainstay. The kids were content and delighted with whatever was put on the table and were never what one could call "fussy eaters." Even powdered milk, which I tried to mix ahead so it would be really chilled, was all right to put on cereal and drink.

We also had about 150 pounds of potatoes and since we were from the Pennsylvania Dutch country, we had been raised on meat, potatoes and gravy for just about every meal. We also had pounds of onions and carrots. They were put out in the garage also and eventually the potatoes froze and we had to eat them anyway. Frozen potatoes get a yucky kind of sweet taste and I had to disguise that with seasonings or carrots or gravy or something. Another food item that I was glad to not have to eat anymore when spring arrived and another lesson learned on how not to store certain foods.

So, we were ready and when winter came, she came with a howling wind, cold and snow. We were used to the snow and cold as we had just come from three wicked New Hampshire winters, where it not only was cold but the humidity in the air penetrated our wool jackets to the very marrow of our bones. The winters in Wyoming had lower temperatures and possibly were more dangerous as the dry air sometimes disguised the actual temperature and one didn't feel it as much. We thought the dry cold was really invigorating although we always made sure the kids were bundled appropriately.

We were in a routine that seemed to work. On most days I could bundle the kids up and send the three older ones out to play in the snow or I could put them all on the sled we had and take them for a walk or build a snowman. After lunch it was nap time for everybody, including Mom. Skip was getting older and sometimes when he just wasn't sleepy, he and I would sit and quietly read a book or play a quiet game. When everyone was awake for the afternoon, it was time for a snack and then playtime till dinner, baths and bed. It was harder to give baths because the bunkhouse didn't have a bathtub, so the two littlest ones and even Heidi sometimes went into the kitchen sink. To give Skip a shower was to turn the water on and have him get all wet, then reach in and with a washcloth scrub him with lots of soap and then get rinsed off. Sometimes, Mom or Dad got pretty wet too. But bathtime was always fun and then our nightly book and to bed.

The bunkhouse had a basement of sorts with some rinse tubs and that's where my wringer washer was planted and I was able to wash clothes but there was only a small space and a tiny line to hang just a very few items. There was a clothesline outside and most of the time when the sun was shining, even though it was cold, if I got the clothes on the line by midmorning, they would be dry by late afternoon or the next day. Diapers and the kids' clothes were primary. The rest could be draped here and there if absolutely necessary, and would finish drying at their leisure. However, there seemed to be fairly frequent times when because of entertaining cranky kids, trying to cook or bake bread, to take care of somebody who didn't feel good or I was just too tired, that I couldn't get the wash done during the day and waited till Karl came home. Then he would entertain while I did a few loads of wash and hung them up at night.

This life was a whole different ball game. After a particularly bad snowstorm that lasted for several days and I couldn't wash, the skies cleared and as so often happens, it turned bitterly cold and the wind was blowing. I had changed the bedding, and the sheets needed to be washed and readied for when we would need them again. I bundled up as warm as I could and prepared to do battle with Mother Nature. When I ventured out, the wind blasted icy crystals across my face and I thought, "This is going to be fun!" It was dark and cold out there, but enough light was coming from the bunkhouse windows to see what I was doing if I kind of tilted in that direction. The sheets were freezing in the wash basket and by the time I got to the bottom, I sort of had to unbend the corners with my own hands so cold it was hard to make my fingers do what I wanted. Eventually, I got them all pinned to the line with my wooden clothes pins. I had hung wash in zero temperatures before and eventually the moisture evaporates and the material dries, so I had a nice feeling of accomplishment as I entered our pleasantly warm bunkhouse.

This night would prove to be somewhat different though. I don't know what the chill factor was but it had to be quite a lot below zero and the wind increased in intensity and I wondered if I had secured the sheets tight enough with my wooden clothes pins. When we woke the next morning, it was obvious that I had pinned everything perhaps too tightly! The only sign of sheets was a strip of cloth approximately five to seven inches wide along the length of the clothes line, secured by clothes pins! The sheets had frozen and the wind had whipped the material with such force that it was the equivalent of folding a sheet of paper, tearing off the large bottom and leaving the rest on the line. The big pieces were scattered all over the meadow with only the small strips still hanging and attached to the line!

I was a really upset mom and ready to cry, thinking all was ruined and didn't know what I would do. Karl dressed quickly and said he'd go and collect what he could. The kids and I watched while he searched for and found the torn sheets with the kids hollering, "There's one, Dad!" and "Look behind you, Daddy, there's another one!" and "Over there, Daddy!" They had a great time directing the big white hunt from inside. I felt really terrible till he came in with this huge armload of sheets and a big smile on his face and said, "Well, I think they're all dry!" Then he went back for the pathetic strips of material still clothes-pinned to the line and brought those in. At that point, the ludicrous sight of those little patches got the better of both of us and we laughed till the tears came. For the rest of the winter we had short sheets top and bottom .

Because John and Elly were gone, we had a quiet and rather subdued Thanksgiving. We did have turkey though, as we could still get to town for an occasional fresh milk, store-bought bread and fresh fruit and vegetables. The storms were starting to deposit more snow and it was starting to accumulate as the weather became colder. About this time the dark wavy line appeared on Baldy Mountain and the elk were winding their way again to the relative comfort and security of the Yellowstone/Jackson Hole country where there was grass and some protection from the severe cold and wind.

Christmas was coming! It had always been my favorite time of the year, and how would we make it Christmas for our family in the wilds of Wyoming? The year before, we had been in Cody in our dumpy little apartment and we had a nice Christmas, but this year would really be special!

We began a monetary relationship with Sears Roebuck and Montgomery Ward, ordering goodies for the kids through the eyes of Santa Claus who just happened to be Mom and Dad. Karl and I were like two little kids in the toy section of those catalogs. And like kids, everything looked absolutely wonderful and would be so much fun to play with! Tonka trucks and army guys for Skip, horses and barns and farms and animals for Heidi, cavalry soldiers and Indians and building blocks and a rocking train for Chris (which he hated, and never would ride in it), and for Eric, stuffed toys and balls and baby stuff, and then books and candies and games and story records and exciting stuff for all of them!

We had to keep in mind our poor mailman who would have to deliver all these things from Cody. Grammy Hahn started sending packages right after Thanksgiving for everyone, including Karl and me. So far, the road over Dead Indian Hill was barely passable, but another storm or two and the truck would have to be abandoned and the snow bombardier put into use. This severely limited what the mailman could bring in to the Sunlight Basin and on over to Crandall where there were families with children who lived there year round. Those people wanted to have Christmas also. We tried to order toys that came in boxes and would be assembled later. Even keeping toys at a minimum, for four little children, it still added up to quite a few packages. I was adamant about Santa Claus finding us. I wished we could share with our children the special traditions that Karl and I grew up with and knew so well, but that couldn't be for a while.

Karl and I had both been raised in a community that celebrated Christmas in its own unique way. I was a Lutheran and he was a Moravian and both of us were very involved with the youth groups in our churches, first as teenagers and then as adults. Christmas was a time to go caroling, to put on Christmas plays, participate in candlelight church services, sing in the church choirs during all those special services, and walk the streets of 250-year-old Nazareth, Pennsylvania, on a snowy Christmas night with the church bells ringing, and absorb the beauty of all the old stone buildings with one white candle in every window. That scene, once viewed, is never forgotten.

Nazareth had been founded by the Moravians back in 1740, who came from Germany. They brought with them the custom of a Christmas putz (from the German word putzen—to show or to decorate). The putz consisted of cleverly done scenes of the biblical Christmas story, right out of Luke and Matthew. There could be individual scenes of Mary and Joseph and the donkey on the way to Bethlehem, the inn and the innkeeper, the shepherds with their sheep and maybe an angel or two hanging from the branches of the tree, the wise men and their camels on their way to the manger in a sandy desert setting, and the manger with Mary and Joseph and the babe, and then maybe another scene with the shepherds and the wise men all gathered round in the manger. Sometimes Mary and Joseph and the babe and their donkey were shown fleeing to Egypt.

Some of these putzes were done very simply with natural

mosses and lichens and hay and sand and twigs gathered in the woods with only one or two scenes. Others were very elaborate with special lighting that illuminated each scene as the story was read from the Bible. And for some families, there would be just the manger and perhaps a few shepherds and sheep and the wise men in one little place under the tree. And in one corner there might be a village with little houses and skaters on an ice pond (usually a mirror) and around all of it, would run the Lionel train with headlight on and whistles blowing! Karl's family had more of a biblical Christmas and my family leaned toward the more secular and commercial aspects.

There wouldn't be a putz for the kids this year as our multipurpose kitchen just hardly had room for a tree, but there would be many others in the coming years that the kids would help build and construct and create on their own. But for now we wanted to instill in all of them the special feeling of peace and joy and happiness that Christmas always brings. We would do our best.

Though all of our children were so very young, we still wanted to have an enchanting and special Christmas even though it would be in the kitchen! I knew Santa Claus would find us even though we were in the wilds of Wyoming! Skip and Heidi were both old enough to pore over the Christmas toy catalogs from Sears and "Monkey" Ward, and virtually everything in them was immediately added to the wish list of both. Chris was two and it didn't take him very long to learn the whole process from Skip and Heidi. Soon he too would recognize and want the treasures that were on every page! By the time Christmas was actually near, the pages of the catalogs were pretty rumpled and dirty and the excitement was growing.

To let them participate in all the wonderful preparations, we began one of our own Christmas customs that year. I had a family recipe for a white cut-out Christmas cookie. The recipe originally belonged to my father's mother and had been passed down to her from her mother, so it was quite old. It was full of butter and cream and lots of eggs and sugar and was a unique and delectable Christmas treat. The recipe made a huge amount of rather stiff dough, so part of the fun was letting all four of them get into the dough with bare hands to squeeze and mix. This resulted in a great-tasting dough even before it was baked! "Please, Mommy, can we just eat it raw and not bake the cookies?!" Just a tiny ball of dough was instantly devoured. We formed it into about nine separate patties about the size of a huge hamburger and wrapped each in wax paper to chill overnight. At this point, they had no idea how this dough would be transformed into cookies.

After breakfast, washed faces, brushed teeth, combed hair, Eric's bath, his bottle and baby food, and sending Karl off to the office, we began our huge undertaking. I had a surprising collection of cookie cutters even then accumulated over the years at Christmas and birthdays. The kids had a great time deciding which one would make the best cookie. Then I got out the powdered sugar and put about a cup in each of six little bowls which contained the colored icing to decorate the cookies. When one tiny little drop of food coloring could turn the whole bowl red, or green or blue or yellow, eyes would get big as saucers and they would grin with delight. Mommy was pretty innovative, so we had some brown and yellow and orange and purple too. There were packages of shiny red and green sprinkles plus chocolate and multi-colored too, which had all been included in the original grocery list of a month ago.

I began to roll out the dough into this huge very thin circle and the three older ones would take turns with their cookie cutters to first dip into the flour and then push down really hard to make a clean cut. I sometimes had to help push so the edges would cut too. Then that cutter would be put down and after some deliberation, another one was chosen and there was a realization on my part, that if we weren't just a little speedier, we would not be done by Christmas, which was about a week away! We had been busy for over an hour and we hadn't baked a cookie! Cutting out the cookies and choosing which cutter, was a serious business. I finally convinced them that we had lots and lots of dough and we could make "gazillions" of Santas, and trees, and stars, and reindeer, and bunnies, and snowmen and bells and all of them! It went a little faster and finally the first batch was out of the oven and ready to be decorated!

Toothpicks were used to dunk into the colored frosting and then transferred to the cookie to make the trees green and Santa's jacket red and his boots brown and the reindeer too, and the bells were all the colors of the rainbow and so were the kids! If someone had warned me ahead of time what a mess I was getting into, I'm not sure if I would've started.

Of course, they had to sample the colored frosting to see if red tasted like red, green tasted like green and so on. The sprinkles were sampled and they licked the toothpicks and their faces began to resemble the decorated cookies with dabs of color and frosting and sprinkles. But what fun they had! And they were so proud of their creations as they were completed! We put the finished masterpieces on a separate piece of wax paper far removed from the work area so they would be safe. We knew exactly which ones were done by Skip and by Heidi and even Chris did some too! Eric spent most of the time on his high chair watching, but he was given some cookie cutters to play with ("Mommy, he can play with these ones 'cause we don't like them.").

By this time I was able to get ahead of them with the rolling, cutting and baking. They were busy decorating and having a fun time with that, so I could just ask "Which cutter do you want me to use?" and they would take turns and tell me, so it finally went quite a bit faster. When Karl came home for lunch, we were not even close to finished. Since so many of the cookies, frosting and sprinkles had been sampled, we weren't in the least bit hungry. Dad fixed his own lunch and watched us while he ate and he had to take his turn with the cookie cutters and the decorating. He was a lot more precise with his colors and the kids got impatient and told him they could decorate a cookie a lot quicker than he could.

Each was given a piece of the dough the size of a large marble and told it was theirs to do what they wished with it. They took turns rolling it out, using a cookie cutter, changing their minds, wadding it up, decorating it, taking tiny little bites of the raw dough, and the one or two that actually got baked came out of the oven looking like they had washed their hands with it, but as Skipper said, "It's OK, Mommy, I can eat it anyway."

Eventually they wound down and it was time to put everybody down for a nap with the promise that they could decorate some more when they woke up. It took a little while to wash flour and food coloring and frosting off of faces and hands but finally everybody had a drink and was tucked in and it didn't take long for all four of them to fall asleep. I lay down with them and wanted to drift off so badly but this was my chance to go ahead and at least finish the rolling out and baking. By the time they woke I was pretty much finished. A little more playing and decorating, then they had enough and wanted to play outside. That was our first time to bake cookies together but we had established a Zeller "rite of Christmas" that continued for many years and there was never a year when it wasn't a fun time for all of us. As they got older, the cookies became really lovely, but somehow I missed the messy faces and the childlike wonder.

'Twas the night before Christmas! Truly! It had come and the three older ones were wound up tighter than a clock spring and ready for Santa Claus! Their excitement rubbed off on Eric and he was happy and full of the dickens too. So we had baths and got in "jammies" and read the age-old tale of Santa Claus and his reindeer and then into bed. After many drinks of water and extra trips to the bathroom and giggles and toys falling out of bed, finally eyes closed and they were in their own "visions of sugar plums."

Now it was time for their dad and me to get to work! He had cut a tree out in the woods and had it stored behind the warehouse. In it came and it was beautiful and smelled cold and fresh and wonderful! We decorated it with our few lights and baubles and it radiated the quiet beauty we wanted for the kids. In came the toys and the gifts and these were placed unwrapped under the boughs and we knew Skip and Heidi would recognize what Santa Claus had brought for them and what would be Chris and Eric's gifts. Some of the toys had to be put together and were quite involved. Karl had to follow directions as to what went where and it was probably 3 a.m. before we were finished. We had designed a fairyland for the kids and in our hearts, it gave to us the warmth and substance of Christmas.

Sometime after 5:30 a.m., Skip's voice filled the bunkhouse with, "Did Santa Claus come yet?" A very tired and sleepy Mommy and Daddy wanted to say, "No, not yet," but we didn't. Karl added wood to the fires while I helped the kids get out of bed and we all headed to the kitchen with Karl carrying Eric. We had not turned the tree lights off and when the three older ones stepped down into that room, their faces reflected the wonder and awe that any parent who's ever seen that joy, will never forget. The magic had come and it was there for all of us and we had a crazy fun-filled, happy, silly, day.

After New Years', Old Man Winter decided we had had enough balmy days and winter came with a howling wind, bitter cold and a barrage of snow. For several days the blizzard continued and there was no point in even attempting to go out. Karl had to bundle up just to fight his way down the hill to the nearby office. These were the days that were long, kids were cranky and bickering and being in the wilds didn't quite live up to the expectation that we had eagerly anticipated.

I played games, sang songs, tried to be patient and understanding but the bunkhouse was just too little and sometimes I lost it and would just sit and bawl. There were times when I yelled at the kids too much and felt truly ashamed of myself. It was one of the many times that I reached for Dr. Spock's book to see if he had any suggestions, although I don't believe that he ever attempted to keep four little children content in a very limited space. Then I would resolve to handle it and for a while it would be better. Sometimes it worked just to take one of the kids and entertain one of them so the others could either play by themselves or just be by themselves for a while. There was extra floor room in the bedroom Karl and I slept in, and occasionally I would let Skip or Heidi be in there by themselves and it was off-limits to the others. And then there were the times when the only way to restore order and my sanity, was with some well-deserved swats on their fannies!

One of the sure ways to entertain them for a while was to give everybody, including Chris, who was still very young, a pencil and a blank sheet of paper. They would all sit at the table and would draw their favorite things. Skip would invariably have a locomotive or an airplane, Heidi would draw her beloved "horsies" and both of them actually did really well. Chris wanted to draw "my guys," which were the little plastic cavalry soldiers and Indians, and his drawings were also amazingly recognizable. He was just a few months over two years old. This was the beginning of another pastime that they were to utilize up into high school age. For the most part, they scorned coloring books and always chose the blank paper and pencils. While they would draw, they would show each other their pictures and there would be a lot of comments (not all of them very nice) on each other's work, and always some laughing and giggling. As the years passed and they got older, the four of them would sit at the dining room table and amuse themselves for hours and two of them became exceptional artists.

But for now, we couldn't do that all the time and occasionally we just had a miserable day. The snow was very deep, it was bitterly cold and there were times when we just had to stay inside day after day. If only we would have had just a little more room to spread out, but we were on top of each other and it was so difficult to do so many things and even keep clean! There were two woodstoves, one in the kitchen and the other in what should have been the living room but was Karl's and my room. Both of them had to have at least some wood stacked beside them so we didn't have to go outside every time we needed to add a piece to the fire. Eric was crawling and pulling himself up and standing and it wouldn't be long before he walked. He was a really easy-going, happy baby but keeping him in the playpen was almost impossible now and the pen needed space too. So if I let him move around, sooner or later he would head for the stoves and I had to be alert so he wouldn't get burned. There was always some ash or dirt on the floor surrounding them. Most of the time Eric looked like he worked in a coal mine and sometimes I couldn't decide whether to laugh or cry at his appearance. I tried to be thankful that there was always enough water and hot water to take baths and showers and keep our clothing clean, but then I would be in quiet frustrated tears. I was getting a classic case of cabin fever and I would beg God to have the winter go just a little faster so we could go back to my beloved Crandall. Eventually the storm would pass and the sun came out and we bundled everybody up and went out and played in the snow.

Karl decided one weekend that he and I would use the Forest Service toboggan and visit old Betty, who lived down the Sunlight road a few miles. I'm sure he was conscious of the fact that I was on the edge of being confined to a psychiatric ward and needed a break in the normal routine. A pair of snowshoes appeared for me and I was told there was nothing to learning how to use them. Karl rang our old neighbor up on our crank phone and she was delighted that we would come. So we loaded all four kids on the toboggan and Skip was told to hold tight to Eric so he wouldn't fall off. On a crisp crunchy sunlight day with a brilliant gorgeous blue sky, off we went! It was incredibly beautiful and exciting to be in the middle of that valley ringed by those huge white peaks! I got the hang of the snowshoes pretty quickly and together Karl and I pulled the toboggan full of laughing excited children. We were their horsies and told to giddyap and whoa. It was a long way, and though I was in great physical shape, the play became really hard work and it was with immense relief that we finally reached Betty's house after a long pull up her lane.

Betty lived by herself and was getting up in years. She had spent all her life in that country and every isolated winter in that valley. Being snowed in was merely a way of life to her. But she didn't attempt to go out and so the only visitors she had either came as we had, on snowshoes or on horseback, and, given the depth of the snow, a horse would have had a pretty rough go of it. In her own abrasive way, she came out and asked, "Are you going to leave those children in the cold all day?" and "I don't know why on earth it took you so long to get here," and "Well, come on, come on, take those shoes off and come in, for heaven's sake!" She had an old ranch house with mostly wood floors and log walls. A red-hot woodstove was going in the kitchen where there was a big rough wood dining table. The smell of fresh-baked something wonderful permeated the air. We soon found out she had made old-fashioned oatmeal cookies ("Hope you like them. Was my mother's recipe.") and soon we had snowsuits and boots draped everywhere, Eric's diaper was changed, and she had coffee for Karl and me, and water and cookies for the kids.

She was a fascinating person with a historically novel life, and I wish many years later that someone had written down or recorded some of her tales. She also never hesitated to let Karl and John and later, Ed know, what she thought of the Forest Service and their "damn policies." That country was hers, rightfully claimed by her grandfather when he homesteaded that country in the 1800s. She was born and raised there and didn't appreciate the U.S. government telling her what she could and couldn't do in that country! A crusty old gal, very intelligent with a heart of gold when it came to kids.

Skip and Heidi were permitted to explore the other rooms but didn't stay long as there were no fires lit in any of the woodstoves except the kitchen. It was pretty chilly everywhere else in the house. We were really enjoying our visit but Eric was showing signs of his missed nap and the kids were getting restless. We had a long way to go and a lot of energy to expend to get home. So we said our goodbyes and our thank you's, bundled everyone back into snowsuits and boots and mittens and hats, piled them back on the toboggan and off we went.

The trip home got a little cranky with Skip not wanting to hold Eric anymore and wanting to know why he couldn't pull the sleigh, Heidi wanting to walk, and Chris tired of sitting still. We finally had to let them try to walk but it was impossible as the snow was way too deep and bottomless without snowshoes. I carried Eric part of the way and Karl was the only "horse" for a while, but finally they tired of trying to make their own way and crawled willingly back onto the toboggan. All was back in order again and we made it home as the sun was starting to go down and the air was turning that heart-stopping cold. It was a great family outing and the little children had no problems going to sleep after a day in the winter air, and neither did Mom or Dad.

One winter day it was obvious that Skipper was really feeling pretty bad and when I felt his forehead, it was hot. He had awakened that morning with a runny nose and complained that his head hurt. I gave him some aspirin and tried to keep him as quiet as I could but his personality always dictated that if he felt miserable, then the whole world was going to suffer too. Heidi and Chris got teased to tears a few times during the day and I was ready to discipline him, sick or not! That little guy could be really a terror, and especially so when he didn't feel well! He was five years old and a pretty big boy who always tried to take care of all of us even when we didn't want him to. He was also determined that the little kids should do what he said! Needless to say, this caused some major problems sometimes. But he was so loving so much of the time and I felt sorry that he felt so awful. I continued to give him aspirin every four hours and lots of fluids and by suppertime, he seemed to be feeling a lot better.

The next morning, he woke up feeling great, ate a good breakfast and soon wanted to go play outside. So did Heidi and Chris. It was cold but I thought maybe a little while would be all right. So out they went and I could keep an eye on them while I took care of Eric and did some chores. But soon Skip came in and said, "Mommy, I'm really cold. I need another jacket on and I don't feel good." His face was flushed and he was hot to the touch! I was really alarmed and took his temperature, which was over 103! He was shivering with cold and burning up! I gave him an aspirin, got him warm and in his pajamas, fixed a comfy bed for him on the bottom bunk of our bed, and called Karl, who came right up. By this time he started to cough, his breathing was labored, and we could hear a tightness in his chest that was appalling. How could this happen so fast? How could he be so sick so suddenly? It was time to call Dr. Stelter in Cody and when I rang the one long for the operator, my hands were shaking so bad I could hardly hold the phone.

The doctor was in and the nurse, who could hear the panic in my voice, put him through immediately. The quiet professional voice asked what the problem was and I calmed down and gave him the information he needed. He gave me a probable diagnosis of pneumonia! I must have started to cry because he said, "Joan, this is why I gave you the unmixed penicillin; for just such a time as this. Now, what I want you to do is get out one of the bottles, fill it to the line with water and shake it really good. Then give Skip two teaspoons now and in three hours another teaspoon and then a teaspoon every four hours through the night and call me again tomorrow morning and let me know how he is. If for some reason, you can't get through, continue one teaspoon every four hours until his fever comes down to normal and then every four hours just during the day. Do you understand what I'm saying?" I told him I did and he told me to also start him on some cough syrup that he had given us and to bathe him with lukewarm water to bring down the fever. We were to try to get him to drink as much water and juice as possible. His last words were, "Now, Joanie, he's going to be all right, he's a tough little boy and he's a healthy kid. Do what I told you and call me tomorrow morning and let me know."

Karl had brought the other two into the house while all this was going on and heated some soup for lunch while I took care of getting the sick bed all set up. The liquid penicillin was a great pink color and must have tasted OK because Skip never even hesitated to swallow it, but the cough syrup wasn't nearly as palatable and some bribes had to be made to get that down. Karl helped get everyone fed and organized and went back to work but told me to call if I needed him. We were both pretty upset, but at least now, I knew what to do and it helped immensely just to be able to do something! For the rest of that day, Skip was content just to lie, drink some juice now and then, and mostly sleep—another indication that he was one very sick little boy!

Through the night we sat with him, and for most of the night, when he coughed, it was from deep in his chest. We sometimes had to hold him sitting up on our laps so he could get his breath. His breathing was so labored and I was terrified! There was no way to get him to the hospital in Cody. The road had been closed for some time and even the mail had not come for over two weeks. It was up to us to give him the care he needed and between my prayers to "Please, God don't let him die," I made up my mind that between God and me and Karl, Skipper would be all right! Period! Finally by morning, his fever had dropped some and his cough was starting to loosen and he could cough up some junk, which made it a lot easier to breathe. He had a long way to go and it took several more days of phone calls to

Dr. Stelter. But after the first day and a half, our little guy truly started to get better and soon was back to his own sweet ornery self. Where did he get the cold out there in the middle of nowhere? None of the other kids ever caught it and we'll just never know.

It's amazing how a life-threatening experience can change your attitude. For at least the next few weeks I reminded myself how fortunate we were to have four healthy, happy, wonderful kids, the love for each other that Karl and I shared, and whatever circumstances of fate dictated that we would end up in this remote and truly awesome wilderness, to share an experience that would soon be a thing of the past. We didn't know it then, but were told later that we and Ed and Patty were the last families to live at either one of those ranger stations either part-time or year round.

Winter moved at its own leisurely pace toward spring and sometimes I just wanted to yell, "Let's get on with it!" There were howling raging storms that came blasting over the mountains and bore down on the Sunlight Basin with all the fury of a World War blitzkrieg, turning everything into a white swirling mass of stinging cold. There were quiet, gentle, soft snows that came straight down and the whole world became a Christmas globe and our little cabin, with its lights on and the family inside, became the contented and happy center. And there were days of deep, almost purple blue skies and brilliant sunshine with not a cloud to cast even one shadow on the white, quiet, frozen world below.

Karl found out that there was to be a big Forest Service Valentine's party in Cody and he wanted us to go. I couldn't imagine how we would do this, but apparently he thought we could and had it figured out. We had become pretty good friends with Ronnie and his wife and their children and we would ask them to keep the kids for one night, which they agreed to do. So not only did Ronnie come to our rescue when we hollered for help, but he and his wife would take care of our children while we risked life and limb to go to a party! We would wear our old warm clothes, take the power wagon and when we got to town, go to R. B. and Jane's house and change into our party clothes, go to the party, have a steak supper, some drinks, dance the night away, spend the night and get back to Sunlight the next day. Mentally I asked myself, "How in the world will we get over Dead Indian Hill at this time of the winter?"

Karl had to clear it with Ed, who made it very clear that he thought we were idiots and so did his wife Patty, but we really didn't care about their opinions. We were kind of afraid that they would want to try and go to and that really would've put a damper on what we wanted to do.

So all was arranged and the big day arrived. Bright and early, we delivered the kids and all their paraphernalia to the Ronnie ranch. They had little kids too and everybody was looking forward to a fun time and our kids were excited, except Eric, who didn't like us walking away from him one single bit! We hurried back to Sunlight, grabbed our good clothes, some food and water and tossed them into the power wagon and away we went. We hadn't had a big storm in quite a while and the snow depth wasn't as bad as it could have been. What an adventure we were on—just the two of us heading up over Dead Indian Hill in the middle of winter—and we had no idea of what lay ahead! We had that feeling that we were getting away with something and that made it even more fun and we laughed and teased like two little kids. We were two "escaped convicts" and this was our flight to freedom!

We had to go very slowly and carefully but the old Dodge

power wagon just chugged along like there was no problem. As we climbed out of the valley and headed up Dead Indian Hill, the snow got deeper and it was obvious the truck was laboring harder but we geared down even further and kept moving steadily along. We really did feel like we were the only people on earth and surely the first adventurers to ever go through that country! It was so beautiful and so quiet.

The top of Dead Indian Hill is an open, windswept meadow with no trees and the wind can blow at gale force across that open expanse. When we topped out onto the meadow, there was nothing to see except a flat, white open area brilliantly lit by the sun. We had to guess the location of the road and I'm sure we were not even on it at least some of the time. The wind was blowing but not very hard. We had only gone a short distance when ahead of us loomed a snowdrift, not real high but certainly deeper than anything we had gone through so far. Karl said, "Hang on!" and he gunned the engine and we hurtled into the drift, climbed on top and promptly settled into the white fluffy stuff before we were able to get all the way through. Karl shifted into the lowest granny gear and tried to rock it or move it even a little bit but we were stuck! Now what? All of a sudden, maybe this wasn't such a great idea, and to be stranded on top of Dead Indian Hill in the dead of winter was not my idea of a fun time. But I hadn't counted on an amazing piece of equipment!

The power wagon had a winch and Karl had spotted some fence posts, the tops of which were white lumps protruding out of the snow. Now we were both out of the vehicle and I helped pull and stretch the cable to the closest post. The loop went over the top and was secured. Then it was back to the truck and push whatever levers were turned or pushed to activate the winch and we began, oh so slowly to be pulled not quite to the post. It worked really slick! Then we could tell where the road was again and would try to continue on our way. So the cable was secured and back inside we went. We made some headway but floundered again in more deep drifts.

There were still some fence posts so I wasn't too worried. Hadn't we just made a miraculous recovery from being stuck the first time? Only this time, the snow was even deeper and the machinery had to work harder, but we were making progress when suddenly we heard a loud crack and the fence post broke! I got really concerned again until Karl assured me there was enough cable to reach to the next post. That time we were able again to make some headway and I stayed outside to watch the whole procedure. We had only ourselves to think about and so far we could turn around and go home if we had to. It was quite cold but we were dressed warmly and for me it was just great to be without any cares except for us and I really didn't care if we never got as far as the party. This was fun!

We would be able to drive for a while and then get stuck again and winch again and we broke some more fence posts and at one point Karl said that there were going to be some unhappy people when they discovered we had wiped out most of the winching posts on top of Dead Indian! It took forever to traverse across that windy stretch and I was fearful at times that our expedition was going to flounder. But we finally made it across and then it was mostly downhill. Even though the snow was deeper by quite a bit in some places, we had gravity to help us along. When we were pretty sure all would be OK, we stopped long enough to eat our sandwiches and drink some coffee from the thermos. Both of us knew that nothing we had at the party that evening would taste as good.

By this time it was late afternoon and we had spent a good part of the day getting as far as we had. Maybe we would be late for the banquet and party. By the time we were almost down off Dead Indian it was getting dark and we could see headlights of cars on the highway. But now we could make better time and by the time we got to the highway, even our road was dried mud in lots of places. We hurried into Cody to J.B.'s house and they had already gone. The door was open and we washed hands and faces, changed clothes and off we went. Had a great time dancing and visiting with all our Forest Service friends, ate good food, and drank too much, or maybe we were just so tired, but we were still running on adrenalin and stayed till the last peep.

The next morning we groaned our way out of bed, hurriedly dressed, grabbed a couple pieces of toast and headed for the grocery store and the Forest Service warehouse to gas up the power wagon for the trip back. By 9 a.m., we had gotten everything on the lists given to us by everybody who knew we were going to try to go to town. I just had to pick up some fresh milk for us. It had been so long since we had had any and I knew it would be a wonderful treat. Karl and I had both heard the wind blowing during the night and there was a good chance that our tracks plus all the drifts we had busted through on our way to Cody had been covered over again. We needed to get going as we knew it would take most of the day to get back to Sunlight.

So off we went, two very tired but happy people who were just a little anxious as to what we would find at the top of Dead Indian. Sure enough when we got there, the wind had covered tracks and created new drifts, so we had to repeat the process of winching and driving, only now, we wanted to get home to the kids as soon as possible. Because we had broken some of the winching posts, there were times when we had to shovel down to where there was still some post remaining. This made it harder to keep the cable from slipping off. But we were able to keep driving for most of the way because we had pushed through the day before and at least we knew where the road was.

It was very slow going and it was much quieter than the trip had been the day before. We were absolutely exhausted but I don't think we would admit that even to ourselves. On we went. We ate snacks on the way and by the time we got down off the hill to the intersection of Sunlight, it was getting dark and when we pulled into the ranger station, it was somewhere around 7 p.m. Ed met us at the gate to pick up his groceries and asked, "Well, was it worth it?" and Karl replied, "You bet!" We rang Ronnie and his wife and told them we were on our way to pick up the kids. They lived down the Sunlight road about three miles beyond the ranger station and we gave them their supplies and our many thanks for taking care of all the Zeller kids. It was pretty obvious that they all had a great time although we got many hugs and kisses. On the way home, Skip, Heidi and even Chris told stories of all the fun things they did.

Maybe it was an absolutely stupid thing to do. I have no doubt that we risked our lives by what we did and it probably wasn't fair to put our children in jeopardy of losing their parents but there are times when, for sanity's sake, you have to venture out and take some chances, and that was one of them. Karl and I, just the two of us, shared another time that we have always remembered and cherished.

One crisp, clear night fairly late, Karl went out to bring in some wood and called to me softly, "Put your coat on and come out." I did and faced the colored heavens! There were green and blue and white and even a hint of red, undulating ribbons of glorious color spread out against the northern sky. They waved and flickered and faded and brightened like quiet fireworks. No one had to tell me that this celestial display was the Northern Lights in all their glory. Karl put his arm around me and I leaned against him and our faces were raised skyward as we watched and were quiet.

On one sunny, absolutely brilliant blue-sky day, I dressed all the kids in snowsuits and boots and mittens and all the warm gear and we went out to play. As soon as we got our first breath of fresh air, I immediately realized it was very fresh! Our noses pinched shut and our faces didn't want to smile! Then I looked at the thermometer, which I should have done earlier, and discovered it was about ten degrees below zero! This was going to be our high for the day! I ran the kids around in the snow and we threw a few snowballs and made a few angels so they wouldn't be too unhappy to go right back in. But this was not a good situation. Frostbite could happen very quickly! It didn't seem quite fair though that we couldn't be outside in such dazzling sunshine!

For the next several days, the sun continued to shine but the temperature would sometimes fall to thirty degrees below zero at night and our high would be from five below to ten above during the bright sunshine day. Then one morning we awakened to the sound of water running! The sound permeated the cabin and Karl charged out of bed and down to the basement to see if a pipe had broken. We looked under the kitchen sink and the bathroom lavatory and all seemed to be in order. Suddenly, outside the windows, we noticed water running off the roof in almost a steady stream! What on earth was going on? Karl opened the front door to step outside and when he did, a gush of sweet warm air invaded the cabin.

Outside there was water running everywhere in little rivulets around the house and between snowbanks. There was an incredibly soft breeze and the air was warm! We were experiencing a true chinook! Karl and I had heard and read about them but to actually have one surround us was phenomenal! Our brains just didn't want to acknowledge what our eyes and our senses were feeling! Was spring here? We didn't know, but I knew that it was time to feed and dress four little kids so we could get out in that unbelievable air! It smelled so good and it went way down inside and made you feel that you were re-energized to the very marrow of your bones.

I dressed the kids in boots and snowsuits and mittens and hats and when we got outside, they went absolutely nutty. They ran and they laughed and we spread our arms out and we were airplanes and flying and having such a good time. Then it dawned on me that it was actually very warm! So we started to peel off layers and the sun got hotter and we took more clothes off and water was running everywhere and it was such a temptation to play in it. Finally I decided we would risk everything and I let them take off coats, hats, mittens, snowsuits and when all we had on was our regular clothes, I said, "OK, everybody, take your shoes and socks off and let's go wading in the water!" Skip and Heidi looked at me like I was crazy but it didn't take them two seconds to get down to bare feet! I helped Chris, took my own off and even held Eric so he could walk holding on to my hands. The temperature had to be in the high seventies and the soft wind continued to nuzzle us and it was magic. We marched through the water in our bare feet and splashed it everywhere, we played ring-around-a-rosey and fell down in soft mushy snow. We even climbed on snowbanks with bare feet, although Mom had to keep an eye out for feet that were getting too cold. There was no question of naps or a rest time that afternoon. I opened all the windows and doors in the house and rejuvenated all the stale wood smoke air.

Eventually, it started to feel cooler and it was time to go in, have a yummy dinner and off to bed. Skip and Heidi and Chris too, had to tell their daddy all about the fun we had and it was nonstop. I don't think anybody was awake when their heads hit the pillows and we kissed them goodnight. That night the chinook moved out and winter came back and the temperature went down to zero again, but it was all right. We had experienced another one of the never-to-be-forgotten miracles of nature and it was awesome.

March had come and there were definite signs that spring was going to come to the Sunlight Basin. We still had some terrific snows and cold but somehow they weren't as threatening and the temperatures didn't go quite so low and we started to hear the coyotes again, which meant they weren't the only wildlife to start moving around. It had been quite a winter and I willed it to end even though I knew in my heart that it would be another month before we could even think about leaving.

I was so very tired of so very many things. We still had plenty of food but it never varied now and no matter what I did or how I fixed dinner, it all tasted the same. The kids didn't mind and didn't seem to notice but I knew that Karl did and there was not anything I could do except prepare what we had the best way I could. I was tired of the taste of frozen potatoes, powdered milk, canned meat, home-baked bread, dried fruit and canned everything! I was tired of the impossible job of trying to keep the house clean and in order, and so sick of wood fires and their mess. I was tired of day after day of trying to keep four little kids happy in too small a space and the monotony of never being able to go anywhere except right around the house when we were outside. I was tired of the other ranger and his wife always letting us know that we could be doing everything just so much better if we just did things their way.

I think that maybe I wouldn't have been quite so negative if I knew that I had to live there forever. But I knew I didn't and I could see "the light at the end of the tunnel" now and I wanted to get out of there as soon as it was humanly possible! I will freely admit that I had a bad case of cabin fever but I still was glad that we had made the choice to "winter in." Karl and I had proved that we had what it took to face the unknown and handle it, maybe not to perfection, but acceptable.

The days were definitely getting longer and the temperatures were climbing and patches of ground started to appear on the south-facing slopes. We would still have an occasional blustery "last try" snowstorm by Old Man Winter, but he was running a bluff. Spring was about to take over and it was just a matter of time. My spirits lifted daily and this was reflected by the kids and all of us were in a much more contented mood.

My thoughts had been on Heidi for quite some time. This was our only little girl and even though Karl treated her tenderly and special, other than for a very occasional contact with Fred's daughter at Crandall and Ed and Patty's daughter Julie, she only ever played with her brothers. I tried to give her that special feeling of being a girl, like her mommy was, and to show her that we liked to be pretty and dress up and fix our hair. But day after day, even though I was particular about brushing teeth, washing faces, taking baths, etc., we mostly reached for whatever old pants happened to be handy, any old shirt and as long as hair was combed, it certainly didn't have to be styled.

Then I remembered that when we bought groceries, I had purchased a home perm, thinking that maybe I would give myself one sometimes during the winter. I'm sure I probably needed one but now I would give Heidi the full beauty-shop home-perm treatment! I asked her if she would like to have curls and I would be the lady who owned the beauty shop and she would be my customer! We told the boys that this was just a "girl thing." So I tried to focus totally on her (with a few interruptions) and made a big fuss about washing her hair and rolling it and she was so excited and giggly! I gave her a mirror to hold so she could watch and her eyes got really big as she held it this way and that observing all that was going on. She was so patient and good through the whole smelly process and I tried to hurry. Finally her hair was dry and we took out the last curlers and I combed it and brushed it and she looked like a pretty fairy princess and I told her so. Then I held the mirror for her to see. She had absolutely no expression on her face and stared into that orbit for a long time. Finally her lip quivered, the tears came and she cried, "I'm not a cowgirl anymore!" It actually didn't hold the curl for very long and taught me never to make an assumption when it came to my children!

To add to the expectation of getting back to Crandall and looking forward to leaving the bunkhouse, was a surprise announcement by Daddy that in June we would go for a visit to Pennsylvania to see all the wonderful families back there! It would be two years since we left and a year since we had seen his folks or mine when they had been here for Eric's birth! Not only that, but we would take the train from Billings, Montana, to Philadelphia and Mom and Pap would pick us up there! Skip was beside himself at the thought of riding and even sleeping on a train!

Before we came West, Pap would take Skip to the railroad yards in Bethlehem and they would watch the engineers put together trains, car by car. This apparently was accomplished by a locomotive pushing cars from sidings up and over a slight hump so they would roll down the hill and bump into previous car hard enough to cause them to couple. This was called "humping." The engineers learned to recognize the grandfather and his grandson and one day, they had taken Skip into the cab of the locomotive and actually given him a ride. So with remembering all of that, he could hardly wait!

Karl had gone one morning to the office to work and when he came for lunch at noon, announced that the road to town was open and passable, and if I wanted to, we could take the car and go to Cody tomorrow! Did I want to?! AND this weekend we could move back to Crandall. This was about the middle of April and as far as I was concerned, winter was over and it felt like the creation of a whole new world! I had been tested and although my grade wasn't a high one, at least I had passed!

That night I made sure all the kids had a bath, washed hair and were sparkly clean. Me too, and we would dress in maybe not our Sunday best, but would have on cleaned and pressed clothes, to go to town! We would eat in a restaurant, go to the dime store, get an ice cream, shop for fresh milk and fresh fruit (maybe some oranges) and might even have time to buy a book or record or a toy for the kids. I was so excited and got everything ready that night. The kids would still have to wear their snowsuits and boots or at least we would have to take them along. I organized crackers and water and Eric's diapers and bottles and all we could possibly need. I didn't know that we were about to embark on the most dangerous of all our wild journeys!

The morning dawned bright, blue sky and lovely. It wasn't long before everyone was shiny-faced clean and ready to go. It had been a long winter for the kids too and as little as they were, I'm sure they felt that their world was getting ready to get bigger too! They couldn't help but absorb some of my excitement! The atmosphere was one of a holiday and it was going to be fun for

158

all of us. Dad was pretty smiley too and helped load up and get everybody in our little green Chevy, which was gassed up and ready to go.

Down the road we navigated and while there was still snow on the road, it wasn't very deep and Karl would gun the engine so we could plow through. Sometimes we would have to kind of slide through and that got to be a really fun game! Karl would yell, "Here comes another one! Hang on, here we go!" The three oldest ones were having a laughing jolly time! We were hoping we wouldn't have to put chains on but had them along plus a shovel, plus the ever-present-in-case-of-an-emergency telephone climbers and headset. On we went slowly but surely; our own version of "over the river and through the woods," but we went over Dead Indian Hill and down the other side. As we crossed the open plain on top of Dead Indian, it was plain to see that the old fence had some freshly broken posts and Karl and I exchanged smiles full of memories. It was amazing how much of the road Skipper remembered and could tell us when we were going down telephone hill and "pretty soon we would be able to see the big road." And he was right. When we could spot traffic moving on the main road, we knew we could bust through whatever muddy puddles where still in front of us and make it to Cody!

As we pulled out on the main road and Karl started to drive about fifty miles an hour, the kids suddenly became giggly and wide-eyed and silly! "Daddy, you're going really fast!" He and I realized that it had been five months or longer since they had been to Cody or in a vehicle on a main road. For them, it was like being on an amusement park ride! Our little wilderness "critters" were experiencing civilization! Eric was now almost one year old and I'm sure he didn't have any memory of ever being in a car! And Chris had reached two years and five months and for him, a major growth period also! Skip and Heidi were just having a ball!

We got to Cody and did all the wonderful things we had planned. We had dinner in a restaurant with real milk for everyone, shopped in the dime store (that was better than Christmas for the kids and all got to pick out a treasure), went to the grocery store, bought fresh meat and milk and potatoes (oh for a mashed potato that wasn't frozen) and bread, and fresh eggs, and that was fun too. By this time Karl had cast an eye to the mountains and I had noticed also that it was getting windy and colder and there were some gray clouds moving in. Karl said, "We better get loaded and get out of here, looks like a storm moving in!" We loaded four happy, tired little kids in the car with all our groceries and purchases and headed out toward home. I t was about two o'clock in the afternoon.

By the time we were almost to our turnoff, it was snowing pretty hard and Karl said, "We can't make it in this rig, we have to go back and get a Forest Service vehicle." So back we went almost the full seventeen miles. When we reached the work center, most of the four-wheel-drive jeeps were out and in use. The best one left was a jeep pickup and we switched our groceries to the back of the truck and covered everything with a tarp. Then the six of us got into that tiny little cab and we headed home again. Now it was snowing in Cody and we wondered what we would find going up Dead Indian Hill. It was still afternoon and Karl was confident that we would be able to handle the snow with the jeep we had. The kids were kind of apprehensive and asked questions like, "Can we go home, Mommy?" and "Is this a good truck?" I changed the subject and we sang songs and talked about our fun day in the "big city."

We left the main road and began the climb that we had made

so many times, but now it was starting to snow harder and was almost a white-out. After several miles, the climb was getting steeper and slicker and suddenly we just slid off the road into a shallow ditch at the side of the road. We hadn't been going very fast so we stopped with not even a hard bump. Karl already had put it in four-wheel-drive and now he shifted into reverse and we backed out onto the road again. I mentally breathed a sigh of relief. But now we couldn't move forward, no matter what Karl tried to do. We could go back, but not forward. He actually was a pretty good mechanic but only knew that either the transmission or maybe a universal joint or something had broken and wasn't going to be fixed that night.

There was no way anyone could have foreseen or predicted that such a mechanical breakdown was going to happen. We now had a problem that was beginning to be serious. By this time it was pitch black except for the heavy swirling snow visible in the headlights. Karl now turned them off as he wanted to save gas and power. It looked like we might be there for a while. I could tell by the expression on his face that he was desperately trying to think of what to do.

Then he said, "I think we're on telephone hill. There's a climbing pole not too far from here and I'm going to take the climbers and see if I can reach Ronnie at Sunlight." It was pitch black and with only a flashlight, he would try to find the only pole that he could climb and it would be slick. I was scared to death for him and tried to convince him that we had groceries and the six of us in the front of that truck would be able to stay warm until someone came along, even if it was a day or two. But he wanted to try and felt it was the best way. He put on all his warm clothes and boots and bundled up, got what he needed from the back, gave me a kiss and said, "I'll be all right." He was going to go out into that howling snowy blizzard which was really putting down the inches. Then he closed the door and was gone into the blackness. Then Heidi's little voice said, "Mommy, I'm scared." And Skipper said, "Daddy's OK, Heidi, he knows how to walk in the snow and call Ronnie, he did it lots of times!" It was good they couldn't see the tears running down my face but I had to smile at the confidence Skip was showing.

With Karl gone, we could spread out in the little cab and of course Skip wanted to sit so he could steer the truck and "make it go." Then Chris, who was already potty trained, said, "I have to pee pee," and immediately Skip said, "So do I," and Heidi said, "Mommy, I have to pee too!" I had just been coincidently trying to figure out how to change Eric's diaper which I knew was also pretty wet. But I knew the other three had to go first and, especially Chris, who was still new at all this stuff. To make it even more "fun," I had dressed rather foolishly with a skirt and stockings and good suede high heels! I had boots along but they were in some impossible corner in the bed of the pickup. So forget that. I gave the kids a lecture on how we had to do this as quickly possible because it was cold and snowy out there. I would help them. I rolled down the window and propped Eric leaning against the door so he could watch us and not be afraid.

I sent Skip and Heidi out the door and told them not to move, then I managed to hold Chris and position Eric, and then Chris and I were out also. The stinging snow hit our faces and it was cold! Skip seemed to be managing his britches okay, so I pulled Chris's pants down and the poor little guy peed forever. Then I got him put together and lifted him back into the truck. I could make a "seat" with my arms and hold Heidi so she could go. I got everybody back in the truck with lots of giggling, and the window rolled up. Now it was my turn! By the time I took care of me, I was pretty disgusted that I had put clothes on that further complicated the process of squatting in the snow to pee in a blizzard! It was really an exercise in patience trying to pull snow-wet pantyhose back, and do you know what wet snow does to a pair of good suede shoes? This was all done in pitch blackness with only the white reflection of the snow to see by.

We were all thoroughly chilled but it was kind of a refreshing thing to do and we were all in better spirits. We managed to reposition so I could change Eric's diaper and then I held him and we all snuggled close to get warm. I had the keys and could have started the engine but I had heard horror stories of people dying in snowstorms because their exhaust had been covered with snow when they ran the engine to keep warm. So before I started the motor I would have to make sure the exhaust pipe was clear and for now, we were managing to keep toasty with five of us in such a confined space. I had a bottle for Eric and could give the other three some water and some crackers and we sang songs and pretty soon Eric was asleep and Chris and Heidi were drowsy. Skip was behind the wheel "driving" the truck.

Where was Karl? Would he be able to find his way back even if he were successful in climbing the pole? What could I do if he didn't come? I couldn't leave the kids. All I could do was sit in the dark and have one of my pleading talks with God, who had to listen to me pretty frequently over the years and who had never let me down. "Please, please take care of him and bring him back safely. We love him and need him so much!" Skip started to yawn, finally quit "driving," leaned back against the seat, and soon he was gone too.

The total silence was broken only by the soft sandpaper sound of the snow hitting the windshield, which was totally covered, and the windows also. I had no way of knowing if we were a covered mound or if part of us was still above the level of the snow. Time wore on and we were in a black void of nothingness that seemed to be endless. Occasionally, one of the kids would move and try to stretch out to find a more comfortable position and start to cry, and I would try to arrange them as best I could and pat them and they would sleep.

When Karl suddenly opened the door with a big smile on his face, my brain wouldn't register what was happening. Then relief flooded my whole being. We had to rearrange everybody and of course now the kids were wide awake. Karl was freezing and wet and brought the outdoors in with him. He made sure we were safe, then started the engine, and even that had a friendly sound. He was back, he wasn't hurt, hadn't fallen off the pole, and he had managed to get through to Ronnie, who was on his way, although it would take several hours for him to reach us. Ronnie had to break a trail through the new snow and although it was letting up, it would still be slow and arduous going. Ronnie would make it, and we would survive yet another adventure, thanks to our daddy who had taken care of us just like Skip said he would!

In the meantime, Karl got warm and then dug in the back of the pickup under the tarp and found some cookies and some real milk that was nice and cold. We had a wonderful lunch while we were waiting. Ronnie came in his big truck and he and Karl transferred groceries and ourselves. I held Eric, Karl held Chris, and Skip and Heidi burrowed in between us and soon were all back to sleep. On the ride home, I quietly thanked God for taking care of us one more time. When we got to the bunkhouse, we said goodbye and our many thanks once again to Ronnie, undressed kids who hardly opened their eyes and dumped them into bed, covered snug and warm. We built some fires, put groceries away, and collapsed. It was about 4:30 a.m.

and it had quit snowing. One of the last gasps of winter but potentially treacherous and deadly, as we had come so very close to discovering.

The new snow melted in a few days and we were busy packing and getting ready to go back to Crandall. Karl had already made a trip over there and taken back some of the things we had brought with us. We said goodbye to Ed and Patty and their little girl and thanked them for all they had done for us during the winter. Upon reflection, Patty had brought us some really good treats and she did offer whatever help we needed when Skip was so sick. Basically, she was a really good person and so was Ed. I was already getting over my cabin fever so the whole world looked so much kinder and better!

To walk into the house at Crandall was a marvelous return to our first real home. Since Karl had already been there, he had seen to it that the electricity had been turned on, the water hooked up and the house was pretty much just as we had left it. It wasn't long before we had beds put together with fresh linens, groceries stashed, a fire burning in the furnace and the fireplace. The kids were as ecstatic as I was and were literally bouncing from the bedrooms to the living room, out the front door, in the back door, down to the basement and back up again, their feet seeming to never touch the ground! We had rediscovered a feeling of spaciousness and room to move!

When it was about time for bed, I had started a tradition of letting them take off all their clothes and run stark naked through the house for several minutes while the bathtub was being readied. This always instigated big smiles and lots of giggles. They would run their hands up and down their bodies because it just felt so good and do little dances and twirls and what fun! I decided to put all four in the bathtub at the same time and just let them play in the water for fifteen or twenty minutes before they were bathed. This practice also made it a lot easier for me. Then it was time for them to be scrubbed, rinsed and dried and put into warm flannel pajamas with feet and then book time. They took turns picking which one. As soon as they got a little older we had two books every night. Skip and Chris would pick one night and then Heidi and Eric the next. Sometimes I read and sometimes Karl read but they always loved it when he read to them as he would change their stories and make them silly. After the books, it was easy to put those little relaxed kids in bed, kisses goodnight, and they were soon asleep. This all happened right after dinner and most evenings they were in bed and asleep by 7 p.m. Then I would do the dishes and clean up and have time to visit with Karl or read a book or sometimes iron or bake a cake and pack a lunch before it was bedtime for Karl and me.

Karl was busy getting his office back in order and the work center and barn ready for the summer season which had already started. The days were getting warmer and now the kids were six months older. Chris had been talking for quite a while and was able to play outside with Skip and Heidi. Eric had just taken his first steps and was starting to say a few words. Skip would be six years old in December. It was time to think about his education.

But first we would go to Pennsylvania on the train! However, had I known how long and inconvenient that trip would be, I'm not sure I would've agreed to use that mode of travel. We had to start from Cody as the Red Lodge Highway over Bear Tooth Pass was not plowed open yet. Our first night was spent in Cody in a motel and then we had to drive to Billings, Montana, and catch the train east from there. We did not have the financial wherewithal to afford a sleeper and went coach. The trains had just developed the new cars that were all the rage with the observation dome called the Vista Dome and these were up above some of the regular coaches as a sort of second story. Seats were not sold on those coaches so the passengers could go up and ride awhile and admire the scenery and then return to their ticketed seats.

If Eric needed his diaper changed or he needed to be washed, I had to take him to the public restroom which was really tiny and manage somehow. There were no disposable diapers so the diapers had to be rinsed out and stored wet until we got to Pennsylvania and the grandparents. This was also true of washing the other kids although Skip was now old enough to go with Karl to the men's room but Karl or I always had to be with some child somewhere. Eric, at almost a year old, insisted on "walking" and got pretty unhappy at being confined all the time. To keep him quiet, we walked, holding on to the back of his shirt because he was just too new at walking to keep his balance in a rolling train car. Skip and Heidi could come and go into the observation car but had to be helped to travel across the open space from one car to another. Chris was also too small to journey anywhere on his own. Trying to get them comfortable and asleep at night was almost impossible and one of them was awake at different times all night.

The two and a half days it took to get to Philadelphia brought back memories of our original trek west and as I compared both trips, I decided I would much rather take my chances in our little green Chevy! Karl and I were absolutely exhausted. He had no idea of what we were getting into when he originally planned this "fun trip"!

But oh well, we were young and it was wonderful to be in Pennsylvania again and see all those great people we loved so much. It had been two years since we left and one year since we had seen our folks. Now we had almost a month to visit and play and have picnics and family get-togethers. All the relatives wanted to have us come visit and feed us! Lots of hugs and kisses and romping and relaxing! In fact there were so many well-intentioned cookouts on the grills that finally, the sight of another hot dog or hamburger got to be a little much!

We had been there for a while and our thoughts were slowly returning to Crandall, when Karl got a phone call from the supervisor's office in Cody! We happened to be at Mom and Pap's house in Bethlehem when the call came. We were being transferred to Meeker, Colorado, effective as soon as we got back and were able to move! It would be a summer/winter deal. We would move out of town onto a ranger station in the summer and in winter, we would live in a house right in Meeker. Skip would be able to start school in the fall. The Forest Service had taken into account the ages of our children.

We were stunned! Where was Meeker? Where was this ranger station, Lost Creek? We would be on the White River National Forest. Where was the supervisor's office? (In Glenwood Springs.) So many questions and our brains were in a turmoil. We had now been in the Forest Service long enough to know that a transfer as often as every two years was not uncommon and it usually meant a step up in responsibility and pay but it meant that we were leaving Crandall and Sunlight! How could we?

We couldn't think about that right then. We didn't cut our vacation short and the trip back on the train was not quite as bad, as we knew what to expect and were better prepared. When the train finally came to a stop in Billings, Montana, we went shopping for enough groceries to get us by for a couple of days and headed for home. We could go via the Red Lodge Highway as it was truly warm weather and the highway was now open. But this time it was a totally different feeling when we opened the door and entered the house that we had come to feel, belonged to us.

Karl headed for Cody the next day to get the rest of the groceries we would need for a while and to get the details of our transfer and when we were expected to be in Meeker, Colorado, ready to go to work. It was now the end of June and Eric had celebrated his first birthday in Pennsylvania. He hadn't even been thought of when we first came to Crandall. When Karl came back he told me we would be packed and ready to go in a week! We still had not accumulated very many personal items and it wouldn't take long to pack and get us ready for the move.

Skip and Heidi were really upset about leaving. Skip wished he could take his dirt pile and Heidi didn't want to leave the horses. I tried to make it all happy and exciting for them. Skipper would go to school, there would be new horses for Heidi to meet, Chris would get a real bed and not sleep in a crib anymore. Eric would be fine as long as he had Mom and Dad.

The kids wanted to help pack so I got them a bigger box and told them to pack all their toys and games. They had to do a really good job because the box had to travel pretty far. They both got that "responsible and important" look on their faces and promised they would. They took the box and disappeared into their bedroom. I utilized every minute of my freedom without children to accomplish more packing, washing, cleaning, cooking, etc. Quite some time passed before I noticed a lot of bumping and banging and dull thuds coming from the bedroom. My brain said, "You better check on them."

I should have been more specific with my packing instruction. Skip and Heidi's idea of packing was to take all of their games and the adults' also, out of the original boxes and just dump the pieces into the big box. We had Uncle Wiggley joining Candyland, liberally sprinkled with pieces of

Monopoly and the paper money covering Eggbeater, Eric's monkey, and Chris's Bullwinkle the moose, Heidi's blankie, Skip's tool belt, and poker chips and cards kind of blended into the whole mix with a lot of other toys! They were so proud of the job they were doing and Skip announced that we wouldn't have to move all those boxes! It really was funny and I explained as gently as I could that it would be OK to put it all back together so we could find it easily when we got to our new house. They gave a big sigh and said, "OK."

When finally we all piled into our little green Chevy and headed down that terrible, awful rutted road for the last time, I couldn't keep the tears from rolling down my cheeks and they just wouldn't stop. I knew I would never again live in a place more beautiful and pristine. Karl and I began our wild journey as two very naive and ignorant but eager individuals who never dreamed we would experience the wilderness reaching into the very marrow of our bones and our beings.

My face was turned to the window so the kids wouldn't see my tears and as we traveled and bounced slowly along, my thoughts turned to the true treasures of the last two years. Our wild journey was ending with so many life lessons learned. We now knew how to get along with a lot less than we thought we needed, how to improvise, how to make do with what we had rather than what we wanted, how to take responsibility for our share of making it work, admitting our limitations and learning in spite of them, realizing that we don't have to be perfect in all that we do as long as we tried our best, looking forward to the next wondrous adventure we knew would be coming, and being able to handle our fears and trepidation and loneliness and come out on top because of our determination to survive and benefit from each happening.

We learned from the all the people we met. There was

strength and endurance to be learned from everyone who claimed that country as their own, long before the Forest Service arrived, and they knew how to give and take from the wilds. We learned that the very wealthy also appreciate beauty and take joy in the simple pleasures of life. We also learned that we had the strength and the God-given ability to forgive others and ourselves for the mistakes that may have caused some heartaches. And in our journey of a wild beginning, we learned that the shared love and concern of a family for each other is the one constant that makes all the rest possible.

Soon after we left that country, the incoming Forest Service wives flatly refused to live at those ranger stations because they felt it was just too remote and dangerous for them and their children. I suppose that way of life is not one that has an appeal for all people. I reflected on this many times over the years and knew that I personally would not have missed, for all the world, the beauty, the joys, heartaches, frustrations, tears, laughter, terror and awesome experience of participating in a world that no longer exists. People change, our ideas change and society is in a constant flux, but the land, the wilderness, and the hills are timeless and they wait.

CPSIA information can be obtained
at www.ICGtesting.com
Printed in the USA
FFOW03n0943040614
5737FF

9 781424 145126